Arts and Sciences

Books by Thomas Mallon

Edmund Blunden

A Book of One's Own:
People and Their Diaries

Arts and Sciences:
A Seventies Seduction

Thomas Mallon

Arts and Sciences

A Seventies Seduction

1 9 8 8

Ticknor & Fields New York

Library of Congress Cataloging-in-Publication Data

Mallon, Thomas, date.
Arts and sciences.

I. Title.
PS3563.A43157A89 1988 813'.54 87-7119
ISBN 0-89919-420-6

PRINTED IN THE UNITED STATES OF AMERICA

S 10 9 8 7 6 5 4 3 2 1

A round for the boys—
Bryan, Derick, Mikey and Mike

One science only will one genius fit;
So vast is art, so narrow human wit . . .

—POPE

Author's Note

Just as the people herein never existed, and the incidents described didn't happen, all sorts of Harvard rules, buildings and curricula, along with other bits of reality, have been tampered with and rearranged in order to accommodate this novel's fictive whims and entirely harmless purpose.

Arts and Sciences

1

Translating forty lines of Greek is hard work in the most tranquil circumstances, but Artie Dunne's task became impossible when, for the third time that evening, the Hedgehog hurled his body against the wall. Halfway through the eighteenth line of the daily forty, Artie's pen went down in defeat. Outside in the corridor the Hedgehog finished his scream, pushed his body away from the bricks and, muttering, continued on down the hall. It was already past eleven, and the forty lines were due at 8:30 the next morning, but Artie rose from his desk, put on his jacket, walked out of Comus Hall and proceeded to Harvard Square in search of a pack of cigarettes.

There were several perfectly good packs right in his room, but after several weeks' residence in Comus he had become accustomed to seizing excuses to escape it. The Hedgehog was one. A graduate student in mathematics, he would pace the halls, clad only in briefs, as he fought for solutions to equations—flinging himself against the brick walls in order to belt a eureka from his brain. Another regular irritant was Voltears, an aspiring Ph.D. in French literature whose real name Artie did not know. Unlike the Hedgehog, Voltears tended to hug rather than assault the walls as he made his perpetually terrified and sometimes weeping way through the dark corridors. He would stare ominously over the third-floor bannister into the stairwell, and two or three times had awakened Artie with 3 A.M. bouts of crying and nose blowing. (A longer resident of Comus could usually quiet Voltears by shouting "Stick a sock in it, you fucking Frog!" from behind another of the dormitory's doors.)

Were it only a matter of Voltears's wailings and the Hedgehog's bangings, Artie might have been able to achieve a bemused *modus vivendi* in Comus Hall, but even its less hysterical inhabitants had a way of making him feel just a bit too creepy for comfort.

There was the incredibly pretty philosophy student who looked like a child from an eighteenth-century painting, a perfect little Gainsborough boy, who was visited on the weekends by his boyfriend, a huge hulk who resembled something the Leakeys had discovered living next door to the Cro-Magnons.

There was Willard Gill, reputedly in his twenty-third year of graduate study (a "23G" in Harvard parlance), a student of ichthyology whose dissertation concerned a fish that had last occupied North American waters seven thousand years ago. Judging from his piscine lack of mustache space between nose and lips, one might surmise that Willard was evolving backward in hopes of meeting it for the crucial interview that would complete the thesis. This eventuality, in fact, was the thing Willard, like many of Comus's residents, most feared, as it would entail ejection from the eternally stagnant pond of graduate study into what was called, with false jocularity, "the real world."

And there was the Mad Doorknob Polisher, a student of Far Eastern languages whose habits lay somewhere between the fastidiousness of a more mannered era (it was now October of 1973) and full-blighted obsession. He had got his name for the frequency and zeal with which he burnished the brass knob and name-card holder bejeweling his door, distinguishing it from all the other dark wooden doors that had been attached to Comus's rooms in the 1890s. He was never seen without a vest, dress shirt and tie. In fact, he was rarely seen at all except for trips between his room and the hall bathroom, in which he would almost hourly fill a little, and very shiny, silver teakettle, and to which he would return almost half-hourly in order to relieve himself of the quantities of tea he poured into his neat and tiny frame.

The Gainsborough boy and Willard Gill and the Mad Doorknob Polisher all lived on Artie's hall, the third floor of Comus, along with Voltears, the Hedgehog, about a dozen other graduate students and, on the weekends, the Pithecanthropus. The third floor was not the most peculiar floor in Comus. Artie knew this not because he had ventured onto the others but because he had one day heard Juan, the Comus janitor, telling Willard, "Is strange, the fourth floor, is very strange."

Artie would have been the first to concede that when it came to new places he adapted badly. He would go to them anticipating brave new worlds, but would spend his first days or months in them sensing doom. When he was six and the family moved less than ten miles, from one small house on Long Island to a slightly larger one, he had nightmares for weeks. Summer camp was wonderful to imagine in April and May; when he got there he threw up a lot. He had spent most of his senior year in high school imagining how blissful it would be to leave suburbia and settle into the Ivy League. In his first week at Brown everyone in his dormitory seemed to get an SDS card, stoned or laid; all he got was homesick.

Things always worked themselves out, even if that took unusual and, Artie now thought, neurotic slowness. In the case of college, he came to love Brown by doing something few people were during his freshman year of 1969–1970: reading. Throughout the student strike over the invasion of Cambodia, he spent his time with Keats's poems and letters, falling in love with the sound of the odes and the smell of the B-level library stacks. The year after that he had friends: Katharine, who loved Shelley more than Keats (or, for that matter, Artie), and who was now a graduate student at Columbia; Freddie, who had kept the dirty secret of his careerism hidden during their Brown years, and who was now in the law school at Harvard; and, most important, Shane (né

Joseph Abbott Manningham, Jr.), the most uncategorizable of them, the slightly drugged Andover preppie/hippie who had become Artie's protector during the strike, bringing him bulletins in the B-level stacks from the chanting, bannered campus far above ground. For the next three years Shane would turn up and go away according to his own unfathomable laws and schedule, but he was the best friend Artie had ever had.

With these few Artie gradually came to feel at home at Brown. Life became less volatile; the apocalyptic strike had given way over the next three years to the current comic death throes of the Nixon administration. By the time the class of 1973 had been graduated last June (without Shane), most of the hippies were looking for ways to get into medical school without having taken the prerequisite courses. Artie had become well educated in writers from the *Pearl* poet to Auden. Rich in his friends and grateful for his education, he left Brown once again homesick—this time for, rather than at, it.

So why, knowing well his own adaptive difficulties, couldn't he just relax until time made Harvard into a good place too? Why not simply sit back and wait for a B-level contentment that was bound to drive away the nerves and the blues? By any fair judgment Oxford Street, which linked Comus Hall and Harvard Yard, and down which Artie was now walking, had a good share of magic and beauty. Lined with glass and brick science labs purring and gestating with machines and mice in the moonlit night, it should have been a source of both peace and imaginative excitement to Artie, but he was too preoccupied with the irritating ways of his fellow residents, and with that most nauseating of questions: *is this really what I want to do with my life?*

It was the question he had been asking himself for the last several weeks, and it was on his mind right now as he walked past John Harvard's statue, across the Yard and out into the Square. *Is this the right place for me?* He was wondering whether he hadn't had the wrong idea about books and knowledge all along. In college those things had meant Keats's lines suddenly blazing into his ken, but now, as someone who was supposed to be committing himself to a lifetime of learning and teaching, he had the terrible feeling that knowledge might, after all, be less a matter of Keats's nightingale than of Willard's fish: something one wearily stalked through twenty years of footnotes with a magnifying glass. Perhaps Voltears's sobs and the Mad Doorknob Polisher's heroic capacity for tea were really the signs of a vocation he just didn't have. Maybe this time it would be different and he wouldn't adapt at all. Maybe he would wind up as just another piece of Cambridge flotsam, bobbing in the Square, from Harvard but not of it.

The Square was very much alive between eleven and midnight. The Out of Town newsstand and Nini's were still open and clogged with people flipping through *The New Republic* and *Nugget*, *The Economist* and *Screw*. Preppie types from the Radcliffe houses dodged the traffic on their way to Elsie's for a last sandwich. The wire trash baskets were filled with discarded copies of *The Phoenix* and *The Real Paper*. Between the columns of the Coop were kids who fancied themselves runaways but were really too close to home, psychically and financially, to be so, playing banjos and pretending to themselves that they needed the coins they were tossed in order to survive.

The traffic lights blinked, the sign above the Cambridge Savings Bank flashed the time and Artie crossed from the newsstand island to the corner of Mass. Ave. and Brattle. A bearded, burned-out figure handed him a card with a poem on it and asked, "Will you look at my work before you say no?" Artie said no, but thanks anyway, suppressing an impulse to ask the guy if he was on the corner because ten years ago he had fled the Ph.D. program in the Harvard English department.

He went into Nini's, waited behind someone checking out with a motorcycle magazine, paid for his Marlboros and then began to walk toward the Harvard Square Theatre in the hope there might be a late movie he could watch until the Hedgehog and Voltears had called it a night back at Comus. In front of the Coop, now featuring a kid of about fifteen playing "Stairway to Heaven" on a harmonica, Artie had a vague feeling of recognition as he passed behind one spectator who was eating an apple and drinking beer from a bottle wrapped in a paper bag. But he went several steps farther before he decided there really was something familiar about the slouch of the shoulders, the tilt of the beer bottle, the hole in the pea coat. Excited, and all at once certain, he turned, walked straight up to the guy and tapped him on the back. With no more urgency and alarm than if a leaf had fallen on his shoulder, the young man turned around.

It was. Shane.

Shane: who played racquetball with Black Panthers; who took him to see professional wrestling in South Attleboro; who wrote forty-page essays on the Medicis; who took debutantes to proms and had them come back the next week to dance naked on table tops at campaign rallies for dorm-mates running for campus office. Who always took care of him.

"Shane!"

"Hey," he said in that low voice incapable of registering surprise. "Urn Man." He smiled. "Where you going?"

"Crazy."

"Short trip."

"No, Shane, really. I'm headed there. You wouldn't believe this place I've gotten myself into. I've been trying to find out where you were for months now. You've been lost since April."

"I've been lost since March if we're really keeping track, Urn Man." He peered down at Artie, who looked little different from the way he had four years before in the B-level stacks. "Hey," Shane whispered soothingly, "as we used to say: whathafucksamatta?" The question contained all the tenderness Artie remembered from years of late-night sessions in which Shane had gently knit up his raveled sleave of care. In fact, it now made Artie feel all the more deprived after seven months without him. "Where have you been, anyway?" he asked.

Shane looked puzzled, if still unruffled. The truth of the matter was that he could rarely recall things like this. "Well, let's see. I split from school, and then I split from Lisa, and then I went around with this chick named Erin for a while. Then it was sort of the end of the summer."

"Where did you go?"

"California. Texas, too, I think. What's it matter, anyway? It was all the same. We balled a lot, did a lot of dope, got bored a lot."

"Why'd you come back here? What are you going to do?"

"A: to check out the folks, filially and financially. B: damned if I know. I'll think of something soon."

"Are you going to finish school?"

"I guess so. There's no rush. That's the nice new little bit of *in loco parentis* that came in when all the other parietal-type crap went out. Now it's 'Fuck who you want, smoke what you want, disappear for five fuckin' years if you want, but we'll always take you back. 'Cause we love you.' We're more like baby bears than ever if you think about it." Shane stopped for a second and smiled. "Anyway, you're the guy with the school troubles, Keatslet. What do you want to wish some on me for?"

Artie made no answer.

"C'mon, tell me all about it," Shane suggested.

So Artie did, as the two of them walked back to Comus with beer they bought at Store 24. There was a rerun of *House of Wax* on Channel 38, Shane said. They could go back to Artie's place and get a buzz on and scream at the good parts.

All the way back up Oxford Street Artie told Shane about the perils of Comus, the yawning pedantry of first-year graduate study and the general jumpiness he was feeling. Shane said nothing or just mmmned as Artie poured forth in a mile-a-minute whisper, just as he always had, sometimes grabbing on to Shane's sleeve for punctuation, practically nuzzling the words into his arm and chest. As Shane opened the green door beneath Comus's turrets, Artie was saying: ". . . and all these old, excruciatingly correct wheezebags quoting Dr. Johnson with such satisfaction and e*mo*tion when you know they'd just about rowf if he suddenly walked into the classroom, with all his bad breath and the giblet stains running down his shirt—"

"Where's the TV room, JK?"

"It's in here," Artie said, turning to the right, "—and some of the acolytes, you know, the protégés who've been listening to all this stuff since they were freshmen in the goddamn excuse-me-you-mean-Yard-not-campus actually wear suits to class, can you believe . . ." Artie's stream of words was stopped by a stream of beer from the can Shane had just popped open and pressed to his lips. "Drink up, and be quiet. The whole gang's going to start melting any minute."

There were four people in the room already watching the movie. Artie gulped some beer and then looked around in the blue-white flickers of light given off by the screen. He didn't recognize three of the others, but the fourth was, amazingly enough, the Mad Doorknob Polisher, sitting very straight and regarding the face of Vincent Price with academic scrutiny, perhaps pondering some East Asian analogue of fiendishness. How odd that he should be here, still in blue pinstripe shirt, vest and tie, watching this lowlife spectacle. And who were these others? From the fourth floor?

Artie felt lucky and safe sitting next to Shane, and after three-quarters of a beer his 113-pound frame began to relax into alcoholic contentment; his habitual hyperventilation began to slow. Before the next commercial he was dozing, only to be awakened by Shane's Olympian belch of pleasure and the clatter of an empty can hitting the rim of the metal wastebasket across the room. Shane shrugged and muttered, "Gettin' old." Artie smiled and prepared to resume sleeping.

9

But suddenly two blue and white orbs flared in the dim televisionary night: the Mad Doorknob Polisher's eyes. Furious, he strode over to the wayward beer can, picked it up and put it into the wastebasket. Then he marched out of the room.

"Where's he going?" Shane asked Artie.

"To wash his hands."

2

Although he had had five and a quarter beers of the six-pack to Artie's three-quarters, Shane had less trouble waking at 7:00 A.M. in the third-floor dormitory than his host. When the alarm went off, Artie felt a sudden queasiness about the twenty-two lines of Greek that remained untranslated. He moaned and squeezed his eyes shut. Shane, un–hung over and mildly interested in the day ahead, said, "Get your ass up, Jack. You've got a class," gently lifting Artie from the bed and dropping him on the carpet. Since one night four years ago when Artie had fallen asleep with nervous anguish on Shane's bed in Ethelbert House at Brown, they had more than once shared the same bed, chastely—Artie with a dim sense of the not-supposed-to-be; Shane with no more self-consciousness than he would have had sleeping with a favorite pet who was inclined to need soothing before falling asleep.

The third-floor bathroom in Comus had recently been remodeled from a sort of 1930s bus-station decor to something more colorful and sanitary. Artie and Shane stood side by side at a row of blue porcelain sinks. The Gainsborough boy, Pithecanthropus-less until tomorrow night and clad in a very small towel, smiled fetchingly at Shane. Artie thought that they were the only three in the room until he heard a quick sequence of gargling, gagging and expectoration coming from someone toweling dry in one of the shower stalls. This would be the Chinese physics student who lived at the far north end of the hall. Artie had got used to hearing his auroral release, but this morning's was so fierce, and he was so nervous about the undone Greek, that he started, driving his toothbrush into his gum and drawing blood. As he leaned over and spat in the sink, Shane patted one of his shoulder blades and said, "Easy, light-winged Dryad. We'll be fifty miles from all this tonight." Artie smiled. They were going to drive to Brown this afternoon and hang out. It would be the first time he'd been away from Comus since September 1.

The cafeteria where they went for breakfast was more the domain of the law school than the graduate school. Part of a neat modern complex designed by Walter Gropius and built around 1950, its Bauhaus straightforwardness was as different from the Gothic labyrinth of Comus as the Harvard University Law School was from the Graduate School of Arts and Sciences. As he moved with Shane from the latter to the former, Artie noticed how the grooming and bearing of the students changed: the slouch of the unexercised graduate student physique straightened into the squash-toned stride of the lawyers-to-be. Long and usually not very clean hair became shorter, sculpted, sprayed and blown; leftover "McCarthy '68" tee shirts disappeared in favor of smart button-downs. Overheard conversation became more corporate, hearty and masculine. "That's a tort, fella," joked one handsome, white-toothed student to another handsome, white-toothed student who bumped him in the serving line. The graduate students who ventured in here for breakfast seemed conscious of their shabbiness and lack of social skills. The only one Artie could spot this morning was Voltears, who was gazing morosely into a barrel of garbage near the microwave.

Shane and Artie looked for Freddie, their Brown classmate from Alabama who had always been a secret careerist and was now thriving in the law school. He wasn't to be found, so they seated themselves near the television to hear the *Today* show's latest rundown of Watergate subpoenas and denials, most of which were greeted by high-humored hooting.

Artie wondered why these aspiring lawyers reacted with such glee, since it seemed plausible to him that twenty years hence a number of them were likely to be in fixes similar to the ones being described on the tube. But it was comedy for them, just as it was for the rest of the country, an amusing slapstick interlude after a decade of Roman tragedy. There was only a little leftover indignation and high-mindedness: "That asshole deserves eight to ten," pouted a John Dean look-alike in disapproval of some prospect of plea-bargaining just tortuously pronounced by Barbara Walters. Artie figured if he asked the guy what he intended to do with his degree, he would probably answer that he was looking forward to working in a reformed Justice Department. If there were few in the room who would any longer say they were preparing for storefront legal service among the poor, there weren't many, either, who would yet admit that the corporate work that was their likely destiny was also their foremost ambition.

But things were clearly moving toward accommodation with the majority culture. Artie had begun to see the truth of the prophecy made by the middle-aged dean who had announced to one assembly during his and Shane's freshman orientation week four years before: "Gentlemen, you probably all think you're pretty special right now. Here you are in the Ivy League, sitting on top of the world you're about to remake. Well, in ten years half of you are going to be selling insurance. And the other half are going to be buying it." The only other pronouncement Artie could remember from that week was one by the college physician, who told another gathering for males only (something already unthinkable four years later): "Young men, I want to put to rest one myth as emphatically as I can. The only way you can contract venereal disease from a bathroom is to fuck the toilet."

Remembering this line made Artie nostalgic as he drank the last of his coffee. Shane, lazily chewing through a Danish, asked him, "So what's on the schedule after Grecian, Urn Man?"

Artie responded, "Well, after I get humiliated there, I'll go to the library, then to lunch and then to the graduate Symposium, where we sit around trying to sound intelligent about the history of English literary styles and ideas. Today it's Pope."

"Before your time, JK. Not your thing, right?"

"Nope."

"Well, don't let 'em scare you. Pipe up on your little sylvan lute or whatever the fuck it is."

"What are you going to do?"

"Check out the bookstores, try to score a little dope, drop in on Mom in Belmont. I'll meet you back in the House of Usher at five and we'll hit the road to Bruno. Okay, Fucker Lucker?"

Cleaver Hall was the heaviest late-nineteenth-century pile in the Yard, a scowling contrast to the neoclassical grandeur of the library and the splendid inevitabilities of the Georgian dormitories. An acquaintance of Artie's in the design school had told him that the most important requisites for any building were "firmness, commodity and delight." As far as Artie could tell, Cleaver had a superabundance of the first and none of the other two, but he knew from the university's self-congratulatory weekly newspaper that Cleaver was the work of an American architect whose buildings—chiefly railroad stations and city halls falling into disrepair all over the northeastern United States—had recently been "rediscovered" and marked for praise, plaques and preservation. In a score of municipalities, perplexed mayors were having to hunt for cash to refurbish the suddenly perceived good taste of their cigar-chomping predecessors in the days of Rutherford B. Hayes.

Cleaver, which would no doubt be earmarked for similar cosmetology, was in the meantime still a workhorse in which scores of the university's courses met each morning; the traffic through its dirty green halls resembled that of a large public high school. Greek 1 met in a small corner room on the second floor. Artie was about half a minute late. As he found his place in a back row, a recitation—first in Greek, then in the student's English translation—was already under way.

" 'τί τοὺς ἐκείνου τοῦ παιδὸς τρόπους ἰδεῖν ἠθέλετε?' Why were you willing to look at the ways of that child?"

"Perfect," responded the professor.

It *had* been perfect, and as Artie eyed the particular child whose linguistic ways had just acquitted him so well, he was struck by the feeling he had every morning in this class: a sense of his own age and senescence in comparison with the others here. Most were undergraduates, many of them freshmen who would go on to degrees in classics. They all seemed to pick up effortlessly on whatever sentences the textbook (an aging production of two old schoolmasters, whose exercise sentences ran to the martial and misogynist) pitched to them. Artie, only one month away from his twenty-second birthday, wondered whether the sector of his brain in which language learning was quartered hadn't already started to dry up. He remembered reading that the male's linguistic facility peaked even before his sexual one—and he was supposed to be already several years past that. The freshmen in here, at their erotic apexes, were near their philological ones as well. Each morning Artie had occasion to rue both his lost high school talent for French and his simultaneously squandered days on the sexual summit.

" 'ἡ παιδεία, καίπερ οὐ γλυκεῖα οὖσα, πολλὰ καὶ ἀγαθὰ τοῖς εὐγενέσι δύναται τίκτειν.' Education, although not being sweet, can bring forth many and good things to the well-born."

Well, that was the problem, wasn't it? A lot of these *Wunderkinder* were preppies who'd had genitives, datives and accusatives stuffed into them like tiny Protestant teething biscuits from the seventh grade of private school through the twelfth. The reverse of Shakespeare, Artie had had little Greek and less Latin: neither had been offered in his public high school, and at Brown he had been too busy filling up his embarrassing gaps in English to get around to classical languages. A reading knowledge of one of those, as well as two modern languages, was required for his Ph.D. He was here in Greek because the instruction was sufficiently intense that two semesters of it would fulfill the department's demand; four of Latin would have been necessary.

With fifteen minutes remaining in the hour, the professor and class were through with the eighteen lines Artie had managed the night before. If he was called on now, he would be forced to attempt sight reading, which was bound to end in disaster. Last week, in a pop quiz, the class had had to translate an uplifting little story concerning a father who summoned his three sons to his deathbed; in the course of his farewell, he said they could find his legacy buried in the garden. They took their leave and, with somewhat unseemly haste, got out the shovels. After hours of digging they had found nothing; but then the bright one of the trio had the ancient Greek equivalent of a light bulb switch on over his head: he told his brothers that Dad must have been trying to tell them something about the dignity of agricultural labor—digging and planting and so forth. Artie, however, did not get the story straight until the next day when the quizzes were returned, his own marked with a dizzying amount of red ink. He'd gotten the father's terminal condition and the deathbed summons right, but through syntactical perplexity and deficient vocabulary he'd had, as the climax of the story, the three sons burying Pop right in the family olive grove.

With that kind of record in impromptu translation, there was only one thing left to do: he began to recite, to himself, as quickly as he could, a frantic decade of Hail Marys. No longer certain of the existence of the ferociously benevolent God of his Catholic childhood, Artie remained a frequent practitioner of prayer. It allowed him to keep his hand in until such time (maybe after his orals) as he could finally sit down and think about the question of God's being or the lack of it. Meanwhile, he still crossed himself when cars whizzed past him at intersections, kept a crucifix in the drawer of his night table and believed that if

God really did exist, He loved him and forgave him everything. So right now he was praying for the Blessed Virgin Mary to intercede on his behalf and get the Father Almighty to stop the imminent threat that pagan culture was posing to one of His shorter creations.

And it was working. The professor, a twinkling, bald-headed man whose brother had once been secretary of state, was resorting to the blackboard to make clear the finer grammatical points of the sentence, "ἡ τῶν παιδίων γνώμη οὐκ ἀεὶ σοφή ἐστιν"— "Children's opinions are not always wise." His explanation brought forth an unexpected series of engaged interrogatives about the nominative plural from two sophomores in the front row. Artie could barely keep his Hail Marys from turning into alleluias. The clock was running out. He tried to look absorbed in the discussion, but was distracted by his own gratitude. In fact, just before the bell rang he turned back several pages in his textbook to a sentence he remembered from the other day: "ἕξει γὰρ ὁ νεανίας ἡδονὴν καὶ τὴν χάριν τὴν τῶν θεῶν"— "For the young man will have pleasure and the favor of the gods"—and with his Bic pen he changed the final genitive plural to a singular—"τοῦ θεοῦ"—"of God." A little monotheistic something to leave as thanks at Mary's feet.

Artie's sense of victory stayed with him through some morning hours at his library carrel and a solitary lunch at Cardell's cafeteria. But it vanished as soon as he entered Warble House, home of the English department, for the afternoon's Symposium.

A snug, eccentric old abode, whose original owner's indoor balconies and mammoth bathtub remained in place, Warble House should have been, unlike Cleaver Hall, a spot to cheer the heart, like Wemmick's little castle in *Great Expectations*. But as he ascended to the second floor, Artie's only expectations were of a low kind. In room 28, on whose spindle-backed chairs and leather couches each class of Harvard English Ph.D.'s spent much of its time, the real spirit of graduate study in the department resided—and that spirit was made of rather stern stuff. Survival was the goal: some would fall away after the master's exams at the end of the first year; others before the climactic orals examination of the third; still more before completion of the dissertation in the God-knows-which. The department chairman had greeted the new 1G's a month before by announcing, "I don't like first-year graduate students. You're all looking for objective correlatives for your neuroses." And this chairman, a thin, yellowed man who had written a book on Chaucer's Pardoner, was considered one of the more approachable senior members of the department.

Professor Wallace Canker, who led the Symposium, was a heavier and less sympathetic man. Disinclined to call on women, and grudging when it came to recognizing those who had not been Harvard undergraduates, he was now conducting the session on Pope's "Essay on Criticism" mainly as a Platonic dialogue between himself and Joseph Branded, a 1G who was both male and Harvard-bred, and who had the further good manners to use his ample floor time to supplement Professor Canker's remarks on Pope with quotations from Professor Canker's book on Pope.

Launch not beyond your depth, but be discreet,
And mark that point where sense and dulness meet.

Artie would dearly have loved to take arms against the grouchy couplets that spoke of "Unerring nature" while cramming it into all those awful ten-syllable corsets. Everything in him knew that one line of Keats's letters, tossed off like summer lightning, was worth a score of these neoclassical fortune cookies, each one more wise and empty than the next. But he would not speak up because he knew that Canker, who regarded as aberrant all English literature written since the death of Pope, would dispatch any protest with another pithy Augustan pellet. He would wait until the beginning of next month. They were scheduled to talk about romanticism then; the French Revolution would have cleared the literary air. Wordsworth, and Keats himself, would be coming on the scene, and Canker and Branded wouldn't have quite so hospitable a thinking-ground for their appreciative squawks toward each other and the text. For now Artie could only wait, and twitch, and drum his fingers against his cheeks.

Despite these vows of patience and silence, he couldn't keep from writhing. It got to him.

> *'Tis best sometimes your censure to restrain,*
> *And charitably let the dull be vain;*
> *Your silence there is better than your spite,*
> *For who can rail so long as they can write?*

Right. But why couldn't he bear it with the same ease as Angela Downing, the beautiful Briton with the cornsilk hair and long legs and freckles? He stared across the room at her smiling self-possession and felt awe: he knew she was no more taken in than he by this sycophantic Boswell-Johnson spectacle Canker and Branded were putting on. Yet where he battled anguish, she felt amusement. She was brilliant, too; he knew that from hearing her speak in the seminar on seventeenth-century poetry they were both in. Why couldn't he be more like her? So percipient, so unvexed, so tall. He stared at her as Branded, in a daring aside, decried the chaotic lack of consensus in contemporary criticism, declared the manifest need for another Pope, declaimed the blessing of having men like Canker in the meantime.

Angela caught Artie's gaze and without the slightest agitation returned him a wide, lazy smile and a wink. Artie blushed and put his eyes back on the couplets in his lap. He maintained this position for a full minute, until a folded note was passed to him. It came via two intermediaries: Elizabeth Bergbaum, daughter of a deceased Columbia professor, olive-skinned, frizzy-haired, caustic, planning to write a dissertation on Defoe; and Richard Marbury, the handsome, blond-headed and sleepy-eyed son of a U.S. congressman, who some days thought he might write a thesis on Christopher Marlowe and others realized he probably wouldn't find the energy to write one on anybody. The note came from Angela. Flustered once more, Artie opened it and read:

Of the twelve men who this stuffy room fill,
Two I'd like to screw, three I'd like to kill.

Artie turned crimson. Was he supposed to reply? Was he one of the two? One of the three? Did the lists perhaps overlap? He looked up and saw that Angela had not altered her relaxed smile; she was still, lazily, looking at him.

Quite unable to answer this peculiar blend of archaism and colloquial diction, Artie made a strong effort not to look at her again, but to concentrate on the class as it limped through its last half hour, the remains of Pope being picked and praised by Branded and Canker and a few halfhearted others. But he found himself unable either to follow the discussion or decide what to do with the note.

The class died of its own dullness a little before 4:30, and as the students somberly shuffled out of the room, Angela approached him. Her powder-blue eyes looked down into his brown ones. "Can you have dinner next week, sweetie? Say Thursday? After Howell's seminar?"

Artie looked up and said nothing, but with his mouth half open he nodded affirmatively to each melodious, Anglo-accented question.

Angela's mouth went into its lazy smile again. "Oh, goodie," she said, tickling Artie underneath his chin. And then, with perfect equanimity, she exited room 28.

Ten minutes later Artie stood in the record department of the Harvard Coop. He didn't want to be late for Shane, so he flipped quickly through the bins for the album by Dan Hicks and His Hot Licks that would be a perfect soundtrack for their time in Providence as soon as they could get a little drunk and meet up with a stereo. At the cash register he joined a line of three other people waiting to have purchases charged to their Coop cards. He tapped his foot to make the time go faster as his mind played scales with the events of the day: his good fortune in Greek, the literary necrophilia of the Symposium, the stunning communication from Angela. It seemed a peculiar mix, but Shane would help to sort it out. With this thought Artie felt an even greater desire for the line to move so he could get back to Comus. *Relax*, he ordered himself. *You'll be there in ten minutes. Nothing can prevent that.* But as he waited behind the last customer standing between him and the register, he thought, *Well, not nothing*. Suppose, for example, he suddenly went up to the display of five hundred Paul McCartney albums set up like a huge house of cards near the escalator. Suppose he just went and kicked the thing down, sending albums flying from this floor to the next. Somebody would come forth and grab him and hustle him off to either the store manager or the police.

It was an absurd thought. Why had it sailed into his law-abiding head? Artie's most serious brush with authority had been getting shushed by the assistant principal of his elementary school for whispering to Darlene Lonigan during an air raid drill at the time of the Cuban missile crisis. *Weird*, he told himself, trying to laugh as the cashier stapled the bag with his record. But the thought wouldn't leave. In fact, as he moved toward the down escalator, he actually veered a few steps away from the Paul McCartney display, as if he were afraid it would somehow draw him to it and force him to knock it down.

Once out of the building, doing a fast trot through the Yard and back toward Comus, he forgot about the odd and, he thought, random fantasy. He would remember it only some weeks later, when he would recognize it as the moment he had entered an alley; the moment life, with which he had always been on more or less ordinary terms, had decided to work him over.

3

Most people who saw the automobile traveling southward on 95 would have said Artie was sitting in the passenger seat. Artie, with his penchant for the dire, would have called it the death seat. Actually, Shane's aging Volvo probably did present a higher actuarial risk than most other vehicles, especially with its owner, prone to hallucinogens, at the wheel, but the car's interior could hardly have seemed more benign as Arthur Dunne and Joseph Abbott Manningham, Jr., approached Providence on this Friday evening in October. Orange light poured through Artie's window as the sun melted like a Life Saver. Between hits off a joint Shane nodded as his friend rattled through the story of his day: ". . . And then all of a sudden, out of nowhere, just in the middle of all this blather about neoclassicism and critical 'tact'—whatever that is; doesn't that seem like just the quality they'd insist on at Harvard, too? I mean, it doesn't matter so much if a book or an idea is good or bad; they only care whether it's, like, discreet—anyway, in the middle of all this comes that note, and as soon as I got it I kind of *knew* it was from her, you know what I mean, but I was still pretty shocked and all, and, well, I don't know, why do you think she sent it?"

Shane, who had already been shown the couplet, said, "I would strongly suspect you're on the A list, Immortal Bird."

"What do you mean?" Artie asked.

"That you're among the naked, not the dead. The to-be-done instead of the to-be-cooled."

"Really?" asked Artie, in a reverent whisper. In all matters libidinous he trusted Shane's judgment absolutely.

"I'd bet on it."

Artie subsided into wondering silence. What mad pursuit awaited him? What pipes and timbrels? What wild ecstasy? He stayed hushed as the Volvo turned off the highway and into the city.

Lieutenant Francis O'Brien, the kindly, bulbous-nosed security guard who had been posted in Artie and Shane's freshman dormitory, had once told the two of them, "Rhode Island without Brown is Fall River." Driving through downtown Providence, one could grasp the lieutenant's geography. The East Side of the city, a steeply sloped hill that held Brown, the city's old churches and scores of nineteenth-century Greek-revival houses, was a splendidly kept secret—the most overlooked place in New England. But most of the downtown was a pit: a few imitation New York skyscrapers, street after street of battered frame houses and a lifeless shopping mall that was really just a "landscaped" old street (down which Shane's car had once slalomed at three o'clock in the morning, with Artie certain they were going to be first killed and then arrested). Their present destination was a little area being gentrified just off South Main Street, at the bottom of the hill. An amalgam of new town houses, old frame ones, dumpy grocery stores and budding boutiques, it seemed to be visibly hesitating in its mutation from downtown ugly duckling into East Side swan. Artie and Shane were heading for the tiny wooden house they had inhabited in their senior year, and from which Shane had disappeared in March.

Artie had always liked the house, and grieved that it would never survive the neighborhood's makeover. Last fall he had lived there serenely with Shane, Freddie, Katharine, Bill (a druggie classmate who had planned to combine the old sixties consciousness with the new careerism by becoming an anesthesiologist) and Boodie. For the last several years Boodie, more formally Paul Reboux, had been the one constant in the house as each new group of student tenants replaced the previous term's. (The landlord, who was absent from present realities as well as the premises, had charged $155 a month for the house, which had come to $25.83 for each resident.) Boodie would stay on until the house came down or was bought by some upwardly mobile type.

Boodie was living proof of the recent rush of history. He had arrived at Brown in 1964 with a crew cut—there were pictures to prove it—and had left in 1967, in the back of a truck headed for Acid Landing, Colorado. After spending that spring and summer chemically moonstruck under the Rocky Mountain skies, he had gone to San Francisco, where he had spent the next three years being "into music" (the harmonica and Jew's harp) and selling belts on the street. In 1971 he had returned to Providence, aged and thinned from dope and macrobiotic food. He never finished school. Instead, he preferred to remain with his cat, Juniper, in the basement off South Main Street, doing odd jobs and reading palms. His clientele for the last activity consisted mostly of graduate students and faculty wives. He charged $5 a hand, which included a rice-paper ink print of the palm. He also did mail-order work: a customer could send in his own ink print and Boodie would dispatch a typed-up paragraph of predictions by the next post. This had been his livelihood for two years now. He had taken the same inward turn as the seventies, becoming settled, sedentary, a worrier about the locks on the doors and the state of the neighborhood, all in all a bit fussy and spinsterish. As far as Artie and Shane had ever been able to tell, he was, by choice, celibate.

Living with Brown students five years younger than himself had been a trial for Boodie. Shane was too unexcitable, Freddie too ambitious, Artie too jabbery and Bill too extravagant with his parents' money. ("I used to have to *work* for my dope," Boodie had once complained at breakfast, like a father who had left school during the Depression.) Katharine, who was sweet-natured, protected him from the excesses of the boys.

Shane worried Boodie especially. Recalling this as they parked the car, Artie wondered whether they shouldn't choose another place to pitch their sleeping rolls tonight. But Shane was confident. "I'll do the talking," he said, pressing the doorbell.

They heard squeaks from the basement's wooden stairway and then the sound of carpet slippers flapping toward the storm door. It opened. Artie noticed Boodie's eyes widen as he took little steps backward. Shane didn't wait for him to say anything. He opened the screen door himself and, as if he were the beadle with Oliver Twist, pushed Artie and his knapsack through ahead of him. "This is your lucky day, Bood. I'll bet some pore of happiness on your palm has been tingling since sunup. That's right, me and little Endymionuto here are gonna spend the night. Just like old times—lotsa laughs. We won't bother the new guys with so much as a whisper. We're just gonna throw these things in the old storeroom upstairs and then we'll be off to do the town. But maybe first, Bood, if you can overcome your own nostalgic emotions, you could brew me and the kid and yourself some of that dynamite herbal tea you used to make." Boodie, swept along on the river of Shane's gall, indicated he would.

"Hot stuff," Shane said. "We'll just stow our stuff and then come down for a nice little rap over a kettle of that good ol' liquid horticulture."

As soon as they were out of earshot upstairs, Shane said, "Well, Jack, the price is right. Let's dump this junk and get settled." He opened the storeroom door. Immediately they heard a long howl of resentment coming from a filthy gray ball of fur that was hurling itself, claws extended, toward Artie. Shane intercepted it.

"Juniper!" Artie cried.

"Always hated this fucking beast," Shane said softly as he scooped up the cat and deposited it in the bathtub across the hall. "Piss off, puss."

When the teakettle whistled, Artie and Shane went down to the kitchen. The clearest memory Artie had of this room was the night Shane had instituted an Armageddon of cleaning, a suddenly inspired move to purge the house of all the accumulated years of student filth and detritus, the generations of junk and dirt that transience will tolerate but vested interest won't allow. As Artie and Shane had sacked the cupboards—which yielded such items as a Wheaties box with Ty Cobb on it and a tin of paprika festooned with NRA eagles—Boodie had protested in panic, "Shane, you're throwing away my food!"

"You mean this shit?" Shane had asked, dumping a plastic bag of furry mung beans into the garbage.

"Yes!" Boodie'd wailed. "These things are perfectly good!"

"They won't be after we start using this roach spray up here," Shane had said, brandishing an enormous can of Black Flag. Boodie, organically horrified, had fled, Juniper in his arms, to the basement.

But now he seemed well disposed toward them, if a little nervous. He tried to make small talk with Shane as they sipped the hot yellow tea. "It's from marigolds," he explained in his eerie, hollow voice.

"And it's great stuff," Shane averred. "So, Bood, how's tricks? Everything palmy in the palm biz?"

"I guess so," Boodie answered.

"You know, Bood, I remember the morning you gave me a freebie right here in this kitchen. You remember how you told me some little curlicue of a wrinkle meant that the sun was destined to play a big part in my life?"

"Yes," said Boodie, wary but professionally interested.

"Damned if this summer my car didn't overheat and die on some highway between Amarillo and Santa Fe, and double damned if I didn't get helped out in my distress by a beautiful little Good Samaritanette who considerably altered an entire week of my summer plans."

"Really?" asked Boodie with a flush of Delphic pride.

"Absolutely," Shane assured him. "Now what about JK here? I don't think you ever did give him a reading."

Artie became a little edgy. The morning Boodie had read their palms at breakfast, he had found a reason to leave the kitchen. Two things about it made him wary: aside from being scared of the future, he feared that God didn't like this kind of psychic horsing around.

"How about now?" Boodie offered, authenticated by Shane's account of his summer.

"I don't think so," Artie said.

"Come on, Urn Man, be a sport," Shane said, picking Artie's right hand up from his lap and offering it to Boodie. Artie squirmed but assented. Boodie looked intently. He pondered. After about fifteen seconds he said softly, "Yooo have small hands."

Shane rolled his eyes. "You get five bucks for this, Reboux?"

"Let me concentrate," Boodie said, not taking his eyes from Artie's palm. "You're going to live a long time."

"Good news, huh?" Shane said, pinching Artie on the cheek.

"But yooo have these funny cross-hatchings right here," Boodie explained, pointing to a spot on Artie's life line.

"What do they mean?" Artie asked, all at once interested in the forbidden.

"Trouble," Boodie answered.

"When?"

"How old are you?"

"Twenty-one, almost twenty-two."

"It could be any time now."

That night Shane and Artie found a number of friends in the Graduate Center Bar, which despite its name was mostly the domain of undergraduates. One of these friends had started Brown before Artie and Shane had, another at the same time and two later; but they were all still in school. In fact, by going through school in the "normal" pattern of four consecutive years, Artie had been rather odd. Most of the students on his freshman hall in Ethelbert House had taken at least a semester or two off. Their reasons were usually drug-related or social-service-minded: Dave

Moody, for example, who'd lived two doors down, had joined the Vietnam Veterans Against the War for some months in 1971, going on protest tours with them even though he had never been west of Pittsburgh. Leaves were never a result of academic difficulty; that was impossible at Brown, which since 1969 had been the Antioch of the Ivy League, permitting students to take any course they wished "pass-fail." Should the student happen to fail a particular course—not an easy achievement—any record of his enrollment in it was expunged from his transcript with Orwellian thoroughness.

The GCB had been the site of one of Freddie's social innovations: the Monday Afternoon Invitational Sick-Drunk Classic. The idea was to drink oneself into oblivion, or at least nausea, on the most socially unacceptable day of the week for serious drinking. Shane had participated occasionally, although he tended to view hours spent this way as a distraction from the higher pleasures of illicit narcotics. Artie had been a spectator once or twice; small quantities of alcohol provoked in him an immediate giddiness. Tonight, after just a few beers, he had to be steadied homeward, down the hill on Charlesfield Street, by a much drunker but much more ambulatory Shane.

The two of them spent Saturday walking along Thayer Street (where the head shops of yesterday were beginning to cede their premises to clothing stores that took BankAmericard), having a catch on the Pembroke Green and sitting on the porch chairs at Faunce House. Late in the afternoon Shane looked up some old friends and suppliers while Artie went to the Humanities Reading Room of the library to work on John Donne. He thought of taking his books to the B-level stacks, but didn't want to befoul his memories of that holy place by bringing a Harvard assignment down to it. He felt estranged from so many of the places he had loved here; he was back but he couldn't get close—like a divorced father seeing his children on Saturday, or a day-release mental patient allowed supervised access to former surroundings. Shane could tell Artie had the blues when he didn't say much during dinner at the International House of Pancakes.

"Come on, Urn Man. Don't tell me you're coming down with that can't-go-home-again shit. Let's see a little negative capability, huh?"

Artie remained inert until Shane threatened to play here-comes-the-airplane-into-the-hangar with a forkful of blueberry pancakes. Then he forced a smile. But, as Lyndon Johnson was always saying when Artie was in high school, he had a heavy heart. And when Artie was blue, he had no talent for counterfeiting gaiety, no matter how socially necessary or just plain considerate that might be. He went back to sulking.

After dinner they started driving back to Cambridge for a party Freddie was giving at the law school.

"Listen up, Jack. If you don't have a good time tonight, I'm gonna kick your little iambic butt from Harvard to Cranston."

"Okay, already," Artie said. "I'll have a good time."

For his hundred or so guests Freddie had appropriated Landon's Inn, a law school eating club, whose walls were hung with portraits of Presidents and Chief Justices, and whose furnishings bespoke a sturdy, brown Anglophilia.

"Hey, O'Donnell, play some Jop," Freddie called to a friend of his as Shane and Artie entered the old frame house. Kieran O'Donnell, a small, smiling fellow, went over to the piano and expertly began belting out some rags by Scott Joplin, whose revival was one of the happier events of that year.

"Hey!" Freddie called out, spotting Artie and Shane. "Let me guess. The Brooks Brothers?" Shane was in a Frank Zappa tee shirt and Artie was wearing something flannel that his mother had picked up at J. C. Penney. Freddie himself had abandoned all his former Brown camouflage; he could now wear his preppy clothes openly, like a Chinese youth after a cultural thaw.

"Dewar's?" he asked Shane.

"Dope," Shane answered, heading to a bathroom to perform his pharmacological toilet.

That left Artie, provided with a beer, to be introduced around. Freddie banged two bottles together. "Hey, everybody. This is Art. Friend from Brown. Big literary genius over in the grad school."

"Whoa-ho-ho," one of them uttered, as the rest offered diplomatic waves. Artie's artsy matriculation made him something of an envoy from the world of culture, which some of these law students, still sensitive to charges of occupational banality, wanted to show they hadn't entirely abandoned—even if it meant bringing graduate students, like unkempt vipers, to their bosoms.

Most of them were, as they were not seldom, drunk.

"Drink up, Dunnie," said Freddie, following this atavistic use of Artie's freshman nickname with some newfound legalese: "Come on over and meet these individuals."

He left Artie with a "1L" who, for all his sartorial indications of prosperity, did chores in return for room and board in the house of a famous professor of government. "Sometimes I think if I've got to spend one more Saturday morning vacuuming those rooms filled with pictures of him and fucking Kennedy, I'm going to pack up and quit school. You ever notice how this whole goddamn university never passed the New Frontier? I guess you don't see it so much over in English, but every place else you get this sicko waiting-for-the-restoration mentality. This guy I work for's wife is worse than he is with all the Camelot crap. She even whispers when she talks, like she's Jackie fucking Onassis."

Artie, who despite exposure to his father's Goldwater Republicanism retained a kind of Irish-Catholic loyalty to the Kennedys, nodded and scanned the room. These people weren't so bad, really. Even this guy was just letting off steam. At least they were *normal*, Artie thought; at least he didn't expect sudden wailings from them, or to see them hurling themselves against walls.

Shane, out of the bathroom, was already making progress. Artie saw him talking to a girl in a Villager skirt and lots of make-up, next to a framed photograph of Helen Keller and Cordell Hull. The girl had closed her eyes, and Artie figured out that Shane was trying to get her to learn a form of Braille by having her trace the ironed-on letters spelling ZAPPA across his chest. "Bingo, baby," he said when she reached a nipple.

Artie looked for a social opening somewhere. Freddie was unavailable, across the room and blitzed, solo-dancing to O'Donnell's second run through "Maple Leaf Rag." A pretty red-haired girl was talking to her benign-looking blond date, and Artie thought he might join their conversation until he heard her say, "Oh, Jesus, Chipper. Grow up. She's just blow-jobbing her way to the top."

Not wanting Shane to catch him unconvivial, he decided after a while to take a walk. He propelled himself, a little high on beer and noise, out of the Inn, going north up Garden Street, past its wooden houses, along its hedged sidewalks. He cut over to the North Yard, went into one of the law dorms and found a folding chair on its second-floor balcony. From this vantage he had a view of the quad's Saturday night serenity. The dorm windows made lozenges of yellow light, behind which he could see a student here, a student there, reading books, taking notes. A few televisions made blue flickers. Someone somewhere was playing a Frank Sinatra record (the law school really was a different world), and a couple were sitting, arms around each other, by the *World Tree*, a modernist sculpture in the center of the quad's lawn that was supposed to be emblematic of international co-operation and looked like monkey bars. A bird's music could be heard somewhere nearer by than Sinatra's voice doing "Night and Day." *Darkling I listen*, Artie thought, closing his eyes. It wasn't Keats's nightingale, of course, but it would do. Artie thought he was almost relaxed. He stayed this way for ten minutes.

Then somebody stuck his head out one of the dorm windows and shouted into the quad, "Hey, everybody! Nixon just fired

Cox! Elliot Richardson's resigned! This is it! The Dick has hit the fan!" The quad came to life: shades rolled up, windows flipped open. Everybody was shouting, laughing, cursing, delighting in it. The place was soon as noisy as a row of tenements on a hot summer night. The lovers unlocked; the girl shouted, "Holy shit!"

Artie shivered, his nerves roused back into action. It wasn't that what would come to be called the Saturday Night Massacre instilled much fear or indignation in him; it was just that this burst of activity made him realize that time was still moving, that things were still happening, that he would not be able to remain quiet, under a calm sky, being soothed by pretty bricks and gates and grasses. The feelings that had been attacking him for weeks gathered all at once in his stomach. He felt the way he had when as a child he had managed to swallow a large ice cube. He had the renewed conviction that something awful was going to happen to him.

He made an anxious beeline back to Landon's Inn.

It was alive with the news from Washington. Political glee mixed with libertarian fear—and the hidden lawyerly calculation that a constitutional crisis couldn't be bad for business. "Isn't it *great?*" Artie heard somebody saying, practically shouting, to somebody else. "I mean, the *nakedness* of it. He's *got* to be impeached now. I mean, giving an order like that to your own attorney general, your own *appointee*. Talk about being hoisted on your own petard!" The room was so crowded now that Artie couldn't see the person being favored with this analysis. He expected to hear some enthusiastic, masculine assent follow. But instead he heard a beautiful, cold, golden, female, contemptuous British accent that he was sure he recognized: "Darling, I strongly doubt that you know the difference between a petard and a potato." She pronounced it, thrillingly, "potäto."

It had to be she. Oh, as the song almost went, it had to be she.

Artie maneuvered himself through a cluster of people in order to make certain. He established a line of sight and then confirmation.

What was she doing here? At the moment, she was looking at the guy who'd spoken of petards as if he were some particularly revolting peasant who'd leapt over the window sill of the Winter Palace. But what was she *really* doing here? That, alas, was clear too. She was with a date: the most pin-striped, chiseled, corporately tooth-filled, GQ-faced guy in the place. A 3L at least. Maybe even an actual graduated lawyer. He was returning to her with a tall, silvery drink. Artie averted his eyes, ludicrously jealous. How, after all, could he think of her as his? One couplet doesn't make a coupling. It just wasn't possible. Anyway, she belonged with, well, that guy.

But he couldn't avert his eyes for long, and the next time they looked up they were met by hers. She raised her drinkless hand and fanned her fingers, golden icicles, in a wave. To him.

He gulped and waved back. And then he stumbled off in the direction of Shane, who was having a contest with Freddie to see who could pitch the most M & M's into a small chandelier cup. Halfway there the press of people blocked his path. Artie stood equidistant between Shane and Angela, looking hopefully, helplessly, in both directions. He had a mad proprietary urge to dash back to her, to embrace her as some terrifying symbol of the present, some goddess of calamity who would preside over all his nerves and fears. But this desire was crowded out by a stronger urge to get back to Shane, to the scruffy past, to the vaguely erotic fraternity that for four years had meant safety.

He tugged on Shane's tee shirt at just the moment Freddie lost interest in the chandelier and lurched toward the bathroom.

"Hey, JK, what say?" Shane asked. "I was looking for you. Figured you'd hopped the viewless wings of poesy and split for a while. What's the story?"

"I'm okay," Artie lied. "How are you?"

"Primo. Nice and fucked-up, courtesy of Bacchus and his

pards. Assuming Bacchus got latter-day domain over amphetamines."

"Shane, are you scoring with that girl you were hanging out with before?"

"You mean the Braille genius? Unh-uh. About ten minutes ago I realized I slept with her sister about two years ago. I don't want to get mixed up with that set of chromosomes again."

"Could we leave?"

"If you want to," Shane answered after a scrutinizing pause. "It might be a good idea, in fact. The way things are going, we may need passports just to cross the street tomorrow."

"Then let's go?"

"Okay by me. Let's blow this popsicle stand."

As they were driving around in search of a Dunkin' Donuts, Shane suddenly grew serious.

"Well, Adonais. I'll send you a postcard from Nebraska."

Artie looked to his left. "Nebraska? What'll you be doing there?"

"You drive through it to get to California."

"California! When? For what?"

"Had a little chat with Mom at the family manse the other afternoon while you were in class saying nope to Pope. Dad has sent word, through her, very gently, that there's no more money for yours truly until I go back to school. No books, no bucks. So, since it's too late to start school this year, and since I could balance all my worldly goods on a bee's wazoo at the moment, I've gotta earn some clams. So I'm going out to California and work for my brother for a year. It's all arranged."

"But you *hate* your brother."

"Hey, what are families for? Listen, Jack, I knew you wouldn't like this, and I hate to leave you now. I mean, I know you're not exactly writing odes to your psyche these days, but I've really got to get out of here. I've gotta get some bread, and, well, I did leave a couple of romantic loose ends out west that I'd kinda like to pick up on. So, when I heard Pop's ultomato, I figured Reaganland is where I'm destined to split."

Artie nodded, but said nothing for a while. Then he just whispered, "Okay."

Neither one of them said any more until Shane pulled up outside Comus. They both realized it was better to say good-bye here and now so Artie could start facing the emotional music of being once more on his own.

"Will you write?" he asked.

"Sure, Jack."

"Okay," Artie said, fumbling with his knapsack. Shane touched him under the chin and turned his head so they faced each other. "Hey, kid," he said in a Bogart voice, "we've still got Providence." Artie laughed. He reached for the handle and opened the door. But his attempt to slide out of the car was stopped by Shane, who swung him around, threw his arms around him, knapsack and all, and kissed him smack on the mouth.

"Don't take any Elgin marbles."

Climbing to the third floor of Comus, Artie was conscious of being drunk and frightened. At the top of the stairs he peered down the hall in response to a smacking sound. It was the Hedgehog coming off the bricks. Averting his eyes, Artie headed down the corridor until his head slammed into something huge and rocklike. He staggered and looked up. He had crashed into the Pithecanthropus.

"Hey, are you okay?"

"Yes, sir," he said. "I'm just going to my room."

4

The next day Artie didn't leave his room until dark. He didn't even go out to get the *Boston Globe* and its account of the Saturday Night Massacre. He stayed inside eating graham crackers and Campbell's chunky beef soup that he warmed up on his hot plate. He was not sick, but he remained in bed most of the day, shivering, falling asleep, waking with a start. He opened up his Greek textbook on the bedspread and tried to get through yet another forty lines, and he tried to map the metaphysical circuitry, as neat as a transistor radio's, of Donne's "The Good-Morrow," the subject of the brief oral report he would have to give in the Thursday seminar he attended with Angela Downing.

He didn't get far with either task. First, there was the noise: Sunday brought no respite from the rootings and whinings and mysterious scrapings in the corridor. And second, his thoughts kept bouncing and deflecting and caroming in an exhausting, ungovernable way, from Shane to Angela and back again to his own unaccountable miseries and fears. Three days ago Shane's absence had been a sad but accepted fact of life; now, after his brief reappearance, it was a fresh hurt. He'd had to live with Shane's departures before, but this time he wondered how he could go on without him. Throwing his books on the floor, Artie slid completely under the bedspread, vowing to think no more about anything. But his mind kept racing, and his body kept shivering, until some synapse pulled the plug on his nervous system and he fell asleep.

For a few hours, anyway. At 7:30 his eyes popped open in the darkness. Thoughts of the undone Greek and unread Donne drove all others from his brain and he went scrambling for his jeans and books in a single movement. Within half a minute he was out the front doors of Comus and on his way to the Radcliffe library, intent on pulling himself together, academically and psychologically.

Once there, he was somehow able to work efficiently until the just-before-midnight signal was given. Gathering his things and heading out onto the street, he felt a little more capable, a little more securely wound. But as soon as he turned onto Mass. Ave. feelings of competence were driven out by an inrush of queasiness and then something like terror. The street ahead of him appeared a great highway of danger and trial. Everything seemed fraught with some sort of disaster he could bring down upon himself. The library books under his arm: he could throw them down the storm sewer, couldn't he? The window of the supermarket: nothing said he couldn't throw a rock through it if he wanted to. It didn't matter that he hadn't the remotest desire in the world to throw a rock through that window; what counted, horribly, was that it was possible, that it was an opportunity to bring calamity upon himself. What was to stop him from throwing a rock into the windshield of the Chrysler passing by? Only, after all, himself. And what was to say he wouldn't somehow lose control and do it?

Artie had no idea what had suddenly turned every window and rock and person into havoc he might ignite. But his id kept racing in catastrophic directions even as his still-dominant superego screamed, *For Chrissakes, enough already!*

As his mind sped up, so did his feet. He walked very quickly back toward the North Yard, arriving on Everett Street with his eyes focused on the sidewalk and his hands in his pockets. Away from busy Mass. Ave., he thought he would calm down. Breathing hard, he walked into one of the law school dorms and climbed the stairs. What he would do is sit out on one of the balconies, alone, just as he had last night, and gaze at the pretty lighted windows, the grass below, the night sky above. When he had a grip on himself he would go back to Comus.

He found an empty balcony and went out on it. He sat down, put his books on his lap, exhaled and looked out into the night. The dormitories were dappled with golden windows. Two typewriters tapped like crickets from different points in the quadrangle. The *World Tree* gleamed in the moonlight. Everything seemed once more serene.

Those flowers near the sculpture: suppose I just went down and started ripping them out of the ground?

"But of course the metaphysical algebra of the third stanza, however compelling it may seem, is flawed by the premise of the second—namely, that love 'makes one little roome, an every where.' For another view, see Keats on the subject of 'Love in a hut.' "

So ended Artie's oral report on Donne's "The Good-Morrow." Each week Professor Herman Howell brought his seminar on seventeenth-century poetry to a close by having the three students give quick accounts of poems of their choosing. He would then appraise each of their efforts and dismiss them—the students, that is, though sometimes their efforts as well. Artie had been the last at bat this afternoon, and his explication was typical of him. Try as he would to stick to technical explanation and historical situation, his criticism inevitably took a tangential moral turn.

"Let me begin with Mr. Clarkson," Professor Howell announced. Artie kept his eyes on him. Once again he noticed how everything about Professor Howell was gray: hair, eyes, complexion, eyeglass frames, suit jacket. He was unnaturally well groomed and composed, a sort of perfect master of containment. In terms of facial mobility and expression, he made Shane seem positively frantic. When he spoke Artie could still hear traces of Mississippi, but he doubted that Professor Howell had traveled more than ten miles from Harvard Yard in the last thirty years. He spoke in paragraphs that ran to the Latinate in diction, the Miltonic in syntax. Among graduate students he was regarded as both terrifying and dull. Asking Professor Howell for an extension on an assignment was like asking an American Legionnaire to support draft resistance. When he lectured on Herbert, even students who acknowledged Howell's brilliance were put to sleep by the droning of his splendidly prepared argument. He spoke so slowly that a court reporter transcribing his words would be tempted to put an ellipsis between each two of them.

But Artie liked him. He found him far more appealing than inexplicably more popular professors like the chairman. Herman Howell, Artie suspected, had a heart, as well as some genuinely passionate feelings about books and life. If he was so deliberately hemmed into his gray perimeter, perhaps it was because he had something to contain, a vitality that might otherwise spill dangerously. Someone like Canker, Artie thought, could afford to affect an absent-minded professor's disarray, because there was no real sap to leak through the cutely frayed edges. Howell avoided all the little tempests of departmental politics, which at Harvard were often a substitute for sex and family. He tended, unlike Canker, to grade a student's work rather than the student himself. He was completely uninterested in the student's background and demeanor. Artie tended to show up at his study with hair clipped into a ponytail, bright red sneakers and stenciled sweat shirts. For all it mattered to Herman Howell, he could be wearing a gorilla costume or a tuxedo. Here the only thing that mattered was what a student could do. It was for this reason that Artie paid close attention to his criticisms.

Looking up from his blotter, Professor Howell was now ready to utter them.

"I found Mr. Clarkson's report on 'Twicknam Garden' to be

intelligent, learned and thorough, a fine balance of the biographical and the textual. The relationship of Donne and the Countess of Bedford was paid useful attention but not allowed to overwhelm Mr. Clarkson's treatment of the poem itself. The comparisons made between Donne's perceptions of Twicknam and Pope's a century later were also rendered with accuracy and utility."

It took the professor nearly a full minute to speak these sixty-eight words. And as he spoke them, John Clarkson struggled not to beam. Think of what all this would mean when it came time to ask for a letter of recommendation!

"I would, however," continued Professor Howell, very slowly, "draw some attention to the style of Mr. Clarkson's presentation. The felicity of his insights is not always matched by a corresponding elegance in his words. There are places where his essay seems, for all its intelligence, somewhat turgid, rather fatty."

John Clarkson, who should have known that Professor Howell took away with the same justice as he gave, no longer had to fight back a smile.

"I would contrast Mr. Clarkson's effort to Mr. Dunne's, which I found pleasantly buoyant, marked by a certain sprightliness of rhythm and diction."

Artie went warm inside. How good it was to hear this! How kind of Professor Howell to notice! Was Angela taking this in?

"I didn't mind any of the vulgar colloquialisms, or even the gratuitous reference to John Keats. We have in the last few weeks observed Mr. Dunne's somewhat alarming tendency to compare lines of fast pentameter to the *brisés* of Mr. Rudolf Nureyev, or leisurely stanzas to the loping home-run laps of Mr. Mickey Mantle. While this tendency might be better controlled, it is not without its enlivening function in the proper informal context. It might, in moderation, even be emulated by Mr. Clarkson."

Artie's scholarship-boy soul fluttered.

"Mr. Dunne's easy style is, however, more likely to succeed where the substance to be conveyed is itself rather light. I think we would all agree that Mr. Dunne had a much easier paper to write than did Mr. Clarkson."

Artie's star dropped; John Clarkson's buoyed. The two of them exchanged looks as they bobbed resignedly on the still pond of the A-minus, the grade graduate students received for just about everything they did.

"As for Miss Downing," the professor concluded, "I can find absolutely nothing in her paper to deserve censure, indeed to deserve anything less than praise that approaches awe. I found her brief remarks on 'Lovers' Infinitenesse' to be a model of perspicacity and elegance, the sound splendidly echoing the sense. My congratulations, Miss Downing."

Artie and John Clarkson looked from the professor to Angela in moony admiration. There she sat in her short woollen skirt and brown sweater and blond hair, probably the closest thing to perfection they would ever witness. Then, before Artie could take his eyes from her, he saw her give Professor Howell an appreciative wink. Artie was dumbfounded: this gesture was the equivalent of goosing Charles de Gaulle, grab-assing Andrei Gromyko. And yet Professor Howell seemed thoroughly undisturbed by this breach of his gray walls. He just smiled as he smiled this time every week, his head starting to vibrate with his own ideas about Donne and Vaughan and Herbert, and said, quite slowly, "Miss Downing, Mr. Clarkson, Mr. Dunne: I will look forward to seeing you next Thursday."

Gathering up his books and jacket, Artie marveled. Who *was* this woman with whom he was about to have dinner?

"He's really rather a sweet old thing, isn't he?"

Angela was referring to Herman Howell. She and Artie were sitting on the sofa in her apartment. She was drinking vodka and Artie was drinking beer, each in mouthfuls really more appropriate to the other's beverage.

"Yeah," said Artie, taking a sip. "I guess he is. Not many

people seem to think so, though. I mean, not many graduate students do."

"Oh, stuff graduate students," responded Angela, who wouldn't be caught dead acknowledging her place among them. "What do they know? A bunch of wankers. One or two of them are deluded enough to find *Canker* nearly bearable. *Really*. He and that spotty altar boy of his make me shudder. Howell, though, is really a soft old boy. I'm sure he still trembles inside to the sound of John Donne before going uxoriously home each evening at five. To a wife who adores him, no doubt. Really, all those withering bachelors like Canker would be infinitely better off if they went home to some nice little wife. Actually, I suppose a lot of them don't fancy women. Well, then, for heaven's sake, why don't they start boffing each other, or take it all out on some pretty little freshman boy who's just come off the farm in East Dakota?"

"You mean North or South Dakota."

"Surely it's all the same place? Anyway, let's not talk about the hideous faculty. Just let me freshen my drink and then we can get down to business."

Artie tried to imagine what she had in mind as Angela went back to the kitchen. He looked around the apartment—this was no ordinary student dump in Somerville or Allston. It was a set of huge rooms in one of the best buildings along the Charles. And the furnishings were up to their setting. Where did it all come from? Artie scanned the bookshelves and found well-bound sets of practically everybody, shelf after shelf, from *Beowulf* to Virginia Woolf, as the nickname for Harvard's freshman English course had it. Back in Comus he had only a few treasured hard-bound volumes amid all the paperbacks dearly bought for the courses he'd taken in college. On Angela's bottom shelves were art books, manuscript facsimiles, antique dictionaries—everything enormous. Artie also noticed two volumes with library bindings and gold letters. One read "Conventions of Rejection in the Renaissance Love Lyric / Downing." Next to it was "Saudi Arabian Monetary Policy, 1964–1967 / Harley."

Artie raised his voice so she could hear him in the kitchen. "Where did you do your thesis on Renaissance love poetry, Angela?"

"At Cambridge, sweetie. For the M.Phil. Years ago. Five, I think."

Artie said nothing.

"I'm twenty-eight, love. And since you're also wondering who Harley was, I'll tell you. He was my husband up until two years ago. After he wrote that thesis, he went to work for Shell for a *fabulous* amount of money. I can't imagine how much he's rolling in just now with all this embargo talk. Think of it—he must be stinking. It's almost enough to rekindle my heart with love. Here, sweetie, eat something," she said, coming back into the room and handing him an oyster-covered cracker.

"There," she said, resettling herself. After a moment or two Artie said, hesitantly, "You, uh, mentioned some business?"

"That's right, darling. I have a proposition to make you."

Artie swallowed; his eyes widened.

"Oh, no," replied Angela, without a trace of agitation, "not what you're perhaps thinking. Although, love," she added, patting his right knee, "I never rule anything out entirely."

Artie reddened.

"No, love, my proposition concerns school."

"Oh. Shoot," Artie said, trying to regain matter-of-factness.

"Well, you're not a terribly good Greek student, are you?"

"That's true," said Artie. "But how do you know?"

"I browsed through your textbook just before sweet old Howell's class one afternoon, when you'd gone to the loo. Really, you do fuck up some of the sentences most awfully."

"I know," said Artie, mortified.

"Well, fear no more. What I propose is this. You give me that book, and I'll translate every last sentence in it for you by Monday morning."

"Why?" Artie asked. "How?"

"Why: because you're going to do something for me in return. How: with great speed and assurance. Darling, I'm one of the few people north of the Balkans entitled to use the expression 'It's Greek to me' in order to indicate ease rather than difficulty."

Artie stared.

"Sweetie, do you require proof? If you'd like I can form the seventy-five irregular verbs in the appendix from memory."

"Oh, no, of course not," Artie replied.

"Good. Because while it *is* quite easy, it's also rather tedious. In the time we'll save I'll explain to you what it is you're going to do for me in return."

Artie said nothing. The expression on his face said *anything*.

"You're going to read—and this is the important part—*and* summarize, for me, all of the awful American literature on the reading list for next May's master's examinations."

"Why do you need me for that?" asked Artie. "It's a lot, but it's so easy. You could probably do it a lot better than I can, in fact."

"You're probably right—no offense intended. But the plain truth is that I simply can't *bear* to do it."

"Why? What's wrong with American literature?"

"American literature, sweetie, is what you read on buses."

Artie received this *aperçu* unquestioningly. Had Angela elaborated, he would have begun to take notes.

"So, is it a deal? I do the Greek this weekend, and sometime just before the exams you give me a complete set of plot outlines, critical histories, influences on and by, and the like. I'll save you from what I'm sure are dreadful tummyaches each morning, and you'll save me from having to read through all of that James Featherstone Cooper and whatever else."

"Fenimore."

"Fenimore?"

"James Fenimore Cooper."

"You mean he's changed it?"

"His name?"

"No. Canker. The reading list. Has Fenimore replaced Featherstone?"

"I'll read the American literature for you."

"Oh, goodie. This *is* a nice beginning."

"Beginning?" Artie asked, once again hopeful of erotic implication. "Of what?"

"Of collaboration, sweetie. I've had my eye on you and one or two like-minded others. Elizabeth and Richard, to be exact. Miss Bergbaum and Mr. Marbury from the Symposium."

"How are we like-minded?" Artie asked.

"In that I'm certain they, and you, like I, have been finding much of what passes for life here to be a matter of hopeless fatuity. You do find it so. I can tell. Don't you?"

"Well, you're right. I do. More and more," Artie responded, warming to the subject.

"I thought so," Angela said. "Well, love, you'll be required to think about it less and less if you'll just go along with a few things I have in mind. But we can talk about that later. Let me feed you a bit of supper now."

Artie left Angela's a little before eleven, unseduced but pleasantly kissed and fed and drunk. He was still somewhat disbelieving about the scheme of exchange—America for Athens—he had agreed to. But the idea of saying no to Angela now seemed as implausible as saying no to Shane. Thoughts of her voice, and face, and plotting filled Artie's woozy head as he walked through Brattle Square. She had told him she intended to recruit Richard and Elizabeth at a party for the 1G's being given by the director of graduate studies on Saturday night. Whatever it was she had in mind, Artie was certain she would bring them into her orbit like moons on strings.

So full of Angela was he that he was able to forget, for a few last moments, that he was a person whose head wasn't quite right.

But then, stepping off the Out of Town News island and walking toward the gates of the Yard, he heard the disaster demons as clearly as if they'd been voices. Suppose he just picked up that bale of magazines and flung it into the traffic? Suppose he shoved that man wearing the baseball cap off the sidewalk right in front of the passing Corvette?

The demons were familiar enough by now for him instantly to recognize their arrival, but they were no less frightening for that. He had been trying to deny that something awful was happening, but each visitation made it more apparent that a terrible dislocation was taking place inside his brain, even as he continued to function through his days. Perhaps, he now thought, he had to face the possibility that, just as one could come down with walking pneumonia, one could get walking nervous breakdown.

In fact, although he didn't yet realize it, he was manifesting an additional symptom as he passed through the gates of the Yard. Absurdly—that was the adverb his still-dominant rationality would have chosen—he looked back over his shoulder to make sure he had *not* shoved the man wearing the baseball cap in front of the passing Corvette. Of course he hadn't, but to the demons themselves had now been added this tic of "making sure."

In the weeks to follow, Artie would learn that it is extremely taxing to check on the continuing survival of each pedestrian one passes while walking around the eighth-largest metropolitan area in the United States.

5

Comatose Hall
October 27, 1973
Saturday

Dear Shane,

A minute ago I was in the bathroom down the hall and heard Blue Boy exclaiming, "What a lovely pattern!" as the Mad Doorknob Polisher rinsed some teaspoons in the sink next to him. A while before that I saw Willard come in the front door carrying an armful of just-purchased loose-leaf paper, Bic pens, Magic Markers, index cards, separators, assignment pads and erasers—I think he even had a new protractor. I guess he figures this time he'll really get it done—which is what I suppose he's been saying to himself once every few months since September 1952.

He probably got the stuff over at the little annex of the Coop they have at the law school. The guy who works the cash register is a West Indian, always smiling and singing and pattering with the customers. He's joyful. After every transaction he says, "I don't charge you for the bag!" and laughs and laughs just like he's never made the joke before. He's the happiest person at Harvard: maybe it's dope or one of those blissy born-again sects you Protestants allow that's done it, but whatever his secret, I'm envious. Sometimes, just to hear him, I go in and buy a newspaper I don't even want. (By the way, I ran into Freddie there the other afternoon. He was buying cologne, pipe tobacco and *Penthouse*. He says hello.)

I guess you haven't reached California yet, but I've gotten your brother's address from your mom, and I hope you find this when you arrive. In the week since you left, life here has gone on in what I guess will be its pattern—oh, God—for the rest of the year. We had another gruesome Symposium yesterday. Canker and Branded went on as usual, making the rest of us feel we were *overhearing* the goddamned class we're supposed to be *in*. And then, about ten minutes before it was over, Canker made some crack about how we weren't participating. Well, he was right: none of us could bear to answer the aggrieved remarks they were making about Wordsworth's idea of writing poetry in the language of real men. They've been living so long on the planet Augustan (ruled by King Alexander the Clubfooted), they wouldn't know a goddamned real man if they tripped over one. The last ten minutes were bearable only because Angela—authoress of the famous couplet—managed unobtrusively to flip Canker the bird when she opened up her pocketbook to get a mint.

Now, as for the couplet itself. I don't think she considers me a candidate for either sleeping or slaying, but we did have dinner. She's the most amazing girl, Shane. (Actually, she's a woman—she's 28!) She wants to do all my Greek sentences for the rest of the semester if I'll read the American literature for her—she simply doesn't *like* American literature and therefore sees no point in reading it. I'll be seeing her tonight at a department party for the first-year students over in Chauncey House (which is mostly inhabited by artsy undergraduate Prufrocks). Angela says she's organizing some sort of guerrilla operation against Canker and that she'll tell me more about it then. She terrifies me, Shane. She's so beautiful and so rich (she's been married and divorced!) and so—I don't know. I can't figure her out. You could.

Something else has been going on since you left. I don't really know how to explain it, either. But I've been having these funny, I don't know, anxiety attacks, I guess you'd call them. I'll be walking down the street and all of a sudden I'll get this feeling, or rather I'll start to imagine—oh, forget it. It's nothing. I can tell you about it another time.

I'm expecting that postcard from Nebraska by Tuesday at the latest.

Yours,
Artie

This letter was wholly inadequate. Artie knew it didn't sound like him. Here he came out in reasonably measured grammatical sentences, whereas with Shane his speech tended to be frantically unsyntactical. The letter sounded like someone whose pulse was almost normal, and Artie knew that wasn't the truth. He wanted to tell Shane he was scared, but he couldn't bring himself to describe the demons—it was too embarrassing—just as he couldn't bring himself to write "Love" instead of "Yours." Before he put the letter into the envelope, he scribbled "I miss you" as a sort of P.S. Then he stamped and mailed it before he could change his mind.

Artie had described the attacks as "nothing." Had they really been that, he would not have hesitated to take the letter across the street and put it in the box in time for the 3:00 pick-up, the last before Monday morning. As it was, he decided not to do that, because it would probably mean at least three "supposes" followed by three over-the-shoulder checks. He would instead mail the letter on his way to the party.

It was a splendid fall Saturday, crisp and blue and breezy with the faint smell of burning leaves on the air. He spent the next nine and a half hours in his room reading *The Deerslayer*.

About half an hour into the party that night, Artie realized that he could hold a position in life even more disadvantageous than that of graduate student at Harvard: he could be such a student's spouse. The females of that species were doubly bound. Loyalty called upon them to make a good impression for the sake of their husbands, like the little wifeys of 1950s organization men, but the renascent women's movement had also pricked their egos into a wariness of being turned into mere "appendages." Even the most wholesomely midwestern of them had maiden or hyphenated names on their lapel tags, and they took pains not to say things like, "Hello, I'm John Clarkson's wife." Instead they said things like, "Hello, I'm Sylvia Mitchell. I work as a counselor at the Mass. General VD clinic," thereby leaving their new acquaintance to guess what they were doing at this party at all. The male spouses had liberal-mindedly uprooted themselves from their own jobs, because it was now the "turn" of their slightly younger wives, who had worked and typed papers while the husbands had gone to school, to train for careers of their own. The new ideological etiquette was less clearly evolved for the males, and they usually introduced themselves in bashful confusion, saying things like, "Hi, I'm John Victor. I'm Cindy's husband."

Artie's heart went out to both sexes in this fix. Here were people, for the sake of love, mortgaging themselves to someone else's future—and what, after all, was that future? Five years ago it would have been an offer to teach at a well-known college as soon as one had passed one's orals and was researching a dissertation. But now the job market was dropping like a dead body through an air shaft. The lucky ones, after they had finished dissertations, and maybe published an article or two, *might* get an offer to teach—without the prospect of tenure—at West Jesus State or Dubious Assumption College in Hurricane, Kansas. The baby boom had gone bust, and for late-Truman-era kids like Artie the bucks would be stopping somewhere else.

Artie had come to the party wearing Hush Puppies, white socks, bell-bottom jeans, a gray shirt, a skinny tie and a madras jacket. This outfit actually made him only slightly less fashionable than some of the other students here, but it began to concern him when Angela approached in a black, low-cut, spaghetti-strapped dress, her hand clutching a small black purse, her hair spilling artfully onto her shoulders and breasts, her face glimmering with health and exactly the right amount of cosmetics.

"You're gorgeous!" Artie exclaimed.

"Why, thank you, sweetie," she replied, kissing him on the ear and tugging his long hair. "But look at you! My God, did the invitation say 'costume required'?"

"Is it that bad?" Artie asked.

"Well, no, not if you're an apprentice plumber in Manchester and it's your big night out. Otherwise, darling, it *is* a bit gruesome. We're going to have to fix you up."

"With what? I don't have any money."

"Don't clutter your mind with details. We'll just go into Boston and make you over. Hush now. Here comes Elizabeth."

Elizabeth Bergbaum was scowling. She looked as if she wore a dress once every two or three years, and on this occasion it seemed as if she'd been forced into tweed underwear as well. "Great cleavage, Angela."

"Thanks, dearie. You look lovely yourself."

"I hate this thing," she began in a thick wurst of Brooklynese. "I stole it from my old boyfriend's other girlfriend when I got pissed at both of 'em a coupla years ago. You tried the food yet?"

"No. It looks revolting."

"The vegetable stuff is to barf. But the pigs in blankets are pretty good. They look kinda like Canker's ears. You want one?"

"I do think I'll pass."

"How about the little guy?"

"That would be you, sweetie," Angela said, poking Artie.

"Oh, yes, please. If it's not too much trouble."

"None at all. In fact, I'm gonna sweep about a dozen of 'em into my pockets for lunch tomorrow. I'm telling ya, with what I'm paying this slumlord on Putnam Avenue, I'm gonna be hooking or driving for Town Taxi by Thanksgiving. Hang on. I'll be right back with the pigs."

As Elizabeth walked off toward the buffet, Angela wheeled

around to Artie, and with an enormous smile proclaimed, "Isn't she promising!"

"I guess so," Artie responded. "But promising of what?"

"Oh, really, love," Angela sighed, in something approaching true disgust. "Will you stop being the slack-jawed ninny? Promising of a little *life*. Of being someone with whom we can make common cause. Don't you see? If a few of us don't band together, living here is going to be like living out some of the more squalid chapters of *Les Misérables* until 1978 or God-knows-when. Now straighten up and cooperate." She grabbed Artie's shoulders and pushed them backward into a more confident posture. The right one let out a loud crack.

"Ouch," said Artie.

"There. You look like an adult human. Now help me out. Let's ease our way toward the left."

Moving left brought them to Richard Marbury, who had just entered, the last to arrive, nearly an hour late. He looked the way he did each time Artie saw him: handsome, well dressed and sleepy.

"Good evening, Richard," sang Angela, extending one hand and pinching Artie with the other.

"Hi, Richard," said Artie.

"Hi, Artie. Hi, Angela."

"Well, Richard," Angela continued. "I'm glad you've gotten here. It's really been rather boring so far. Hasn't it been, Arthur?" Angela glared. "I said, hasn't it been rather boring?"

Artie started. "Oh. Yes. Boring. It's been."

"See, Richard," Angela smiled, turning her gaze to Congressman Marbury's son. "It *has* been boring. In fact, some of them seem to take that 'religious vocation' business rather literally."

"Religious vocation?" Richard asked.

"Yes, don't you remember? That letter the department sent out this summer along with the M.A. reading list. The one which compared the graduate study of literature to a religious calling.

It rather made me wonder if we weren't going to be issued little self-mortifying whips upon arrival."

Richard laughed. "I don't think I read the letter. In fact, I don't think I have the reading list. When are the exams, anyway?"

"They're in May, darling. Don't worry. We'll get you ready for them. Oh, look, why don't you go over and give Elizabeth a hand? She's carrying rather a lot of those pigs in afghans or whatever they are. I suspect she has four or five to spare for you."

Richard went to Elizabeth's aid.

"There, love," Angela said to Artie, beaming again. "Even better than I expected. Doesn't even read the mail the place sends. Isn't he just fine?"

Artie smiled lamely.

Angela interjected, "No, let me guess. You're going to say"—and here she switched into a cloddishly atonal American accent—"I guess so."

Artie laughed and fidgeted.

"Darling, why don't you relieve yourself in the loo? Yours is rather a nervous little bladder, if I recall Thursday's dinner. I'll see to things with Elizabeth and Richard. Don't worry. I'll save you a piggie."

"Okay," Artie said. The truth was, he did have to go to the bathroom, not only to urinate but to wipe cold sweat from his forehead. Angela didn't know about the one-sided conversation going on in his head: suppose he just threw the punch bowl on the floor? Suppose he just broke the window in front of which Branded and Canker were marveling at each other? Suppose he pushed Sylvia Mitchell of the Mass. General VD clinic right into the fireplace? This was the first time the demons had presented themselves while he was among people he knew. Returning from the bathroom, he found his legs were shaking.

Angela certainly had Elizabeth and Richard under control. She was entertaining them near the piano, probably searching for more hints of nihilism in their conversation. Artie, hands in pockets and ready to look over his shoulder whenever necessary, went over to a couch and sat down by himself. He tried to regulate his breathing and fight the desire to flee. He managed to stay where he was for nearly a half hour, during which time three different people attempted to engage him in conversation. The first of these was a milkmaidish girl with enormous eyes and flowing hair and great gobs of blush-on, whose ample figure was covered by a sort of dirndl, and whom he would only remember saying, "My dream is to write a book about Dylan Thomas. He was such a *wonderful* poet. Such a wonderful *soul.*" She had been an undergraduate at Bard. The second was a dark, brooding figure who reminded Artie of one of the less pleasant boys in *Lord of the Flies*. "What quintile do you expect to make on medieval?" he asked. The last of the three was a well-mannered and good-looking assistant professor named Jeffrey Stanhope, who smiled at Artie and asked if he could fill his glass. When Artie said yes, please, Jeffrey Stanhope said softly, "I'll bet if I asked you what you were having, you'd say what Dorothy Parker supposedly said when someone asked her that."

"What was that?" Artie asked.

" 'Not much fun,' " Jeffrey quoted, smiling. When he returned with Artie's drink, he patted him on the shoulder, and sensing he would rather be by himself, smiled and went off.

Not long after this Artie left, pausing on the front steps of Chauncey House to breathe in some air and sky and stars before starting off on what he knew would be the tormenting obstacle course home. Before he could step down to the sidewalk, someone grabbed him by the elbow and swung him around.

"You've had a perfectly rotten time," Angela said, more in accusation than sympathy.

"I guess so," Artie said, mimicking her earlier mimicry of him. "You seemed to be having a good time with Elizabeth and Richard. Especially Richard."

"Well, thank the Lord! Jealousy! An almost human reaction!

A reflex—rather primitive, but a sign that the patient is alive. And here I thought you were just a bit of taxidermy dressed up in those ridiculous rags."

Artie couldn't help laughing at her. He wished they could stand here all night so she could tease him and let her endlessly melodic Anglo-syntactical phrases wash over him and keep him from the lunatic fears that lay between Chauncey and Comus.

As a matter of fact, Angela did take him in her arms and kiss him. She stroked his hair. And when their lips parted, she drew his face back up toward hers and whispered, in a tone unlike any he had yet heard her speak, "I know something's wrong, love. Do hang on. It will get better."

Artie swallowed with sudden emotion.

"Don't say a word," Angela commanded softly. "Just take my word for it. And be at my flat on Monday at five-thirty. Elizabeth and Richard will be there too."

Artie nodded and started for Comus.

When in the grip of the demons, Artie was of course too preoccupied to keep statistics. But an omniscient observer—say, the God he still half believed in—could have told him that by the time he made it through the Square and then the Yard and finally to the benches outside the new Science Center, where he sat down, drained of energy and will, he had imagined calamities of his own instigation involving no fewer than twelve human beings, three automobiles, five plate glass windows, two bicycles and one dog. Within seven minutes and forty seconds he had not once removed his hands from his pockets and had looked over his shoulder twenty-three times.

He was more than discouraged. He was terrified. He thought he might pass out.

He tried to imagine Angela's kiss of eight minutes ago. He could recall the charge that had made the hairs on his shins stand up, and his surprise, but he could not have said that it was unlike anything else he had ever experienced. In fact, he had had the very same sensations when Shane kissed him last Saturday night in the Volvo.

This sense of correspondence occasioned further trouble in Artie's already troubled brain. More than once during the last four years he had had to ask himself whether he wasn't in love with Shane. What, after all, was one supposed to call the kind of excitement, surrender and dependence Shane had always provoked in him? Artie had always been able to reason himself away from the unwanted answer. But what about now: what could he conclude about himself and Angela?

Artie was not without erotic experience. He had been involved in sexual activity seven times. For this statistic an omniscient observer would have been superfluous; Artie knew the figure himself. The first time had actually been the most orgiastic—the occasion involving six persons, all the same sex, at a Cub Scout jamboree; Artie had spent most of the three minutes of the experience's duration looking at the eleven-year-old on his right in order to see what he was supposed to do next. The second through fifth occasions had come several years later, while he was a sophomore at Brown, with a free-spirited anthropology major who found Artie "sort of interesting" and going to bed with him "sort of fun." Artie knew she was enjoying this sort of fun with several other males, some of them acquaintances of his, on different evenings. And while the activity had been surprisingly satisfactory for both him and the girl, he had been the party to terminate it, because it hadn't felt right—that is to say, he hadn't felt anything above the neck, however delightful had been his sensations below the waist.

The final two occasions had been with Katharine, the lover of Shelley, in the room above Boodie's lair in the house off South Main Street. Artie had been substantially engaged above the neck, Katharine somewhat less so. Below the waist things had been less than fulfilling for both of them, and after two tries they had called it quits.

Memories of these experiences diverted Artie's attention from the demons for a minute or two, but no more than that. He knew he was in a crisis. He had been sleeping little, eating hardly at all. Looking straight ahead, he could see Memorial Hall, Harvard's startling Gothic monument to its Civil War dead. The other day he had given blood there during one of the university's vigorous drives. He had made the 110-pound cutoff weight for donors by eleven ounces. After lying on a stretcher beneath a stained glass window depicting Andromache, and watching the unoxygenated purple fluid leave his arm and enter a plastic bag, he had been put back on his feet by a volunteer, only to collapse on his way to the table of restorative juice and cookies.

Something had to be done. But nothing seemed to offer plausible help. Four years ago he would have disappeared into his work, as he suspected some of the homesick freshmen "wonking" away in the Science Center library were doing right now. But this was an emergency that seemed beyond the healing powers of both Keats and the B-level stacks, or whatever their Harvard equivalents might be.

Hopelessly, he got up from the bench and walked toward Comus. The lateness of the hour and the scarceness of pedestrians allowed him to reach home with only two more "supposes" and their over-the-shoulder checks. Arriving on the third floor, he was called to by the Gainsborough boy: "Oh, Artie! Someone named Shane called you."

"Did he leave a number? Or a message?" Artie asked quickly.

"No. Sorry."

"Did he say where he was calling from?"

"No. Not that either. He had a really sexy voice, though."

6

Artie spent all of Sunday inside, subsisting on oranges and toast and smoking a lot as he read, for the summary he'd promised Angela, Whitman's hymns to America's outdoorsy confidence.

Angela, for her part, was as good as her word. As Artie emerged, pale and shaky, from his room in Comus at 8:15 A.M. on Monday, the Pithecanthropus, departing for his work week after a goodbye kiss from the Gainsborough boy, handed him a book. "Some lady came by with this about an hour ago. She asked me if I'd hold on to it 'til you got up. She didn't want to wake you." Artie took the Greek text and thanked him.

Walking to Cleaver, he resisted opening it to see whether Angela had accomplished the entire project. He kept his eyes on his shoes and his mind on the walkways in an attempt to screen out of his catastrophic imagination the hundreds of early-morning pedestrians traversing Oxford Street and the Yard. By the time he slipped into his seat in class, he was bathed in the cold sweat that had become the demons' usual host environment. Only then did he open the book to find that Angela had translated every single sentence, without revision, on her first try; she had even used ink. What's more, she had gone back and corrected all of his mistakes for the past two months. She had even annotated some of the text's aphoristic examples, with comments ranging from "Rubbish" to "Reminiscent of my ex-husband." She had defaced the illustrations of heroes and pottery with mustaches and cracks, and on the lesson for today's class she had written a note: "Cheer up, sweetie. See you at five-thirty."

Artie was the third person to be called on. He mouthed Angela's translation still with no idea what half the Greek words meant. The professor responded, "Impeccable, Mr. Dunne."

Artie felt a twinge of conscience. This was the class in which ten days ago he had been reciting Hail Marys; now here he was breaking a corollary of the seventh commandment and ready to do so every day for the rest of the year. Of course, he would still have to take the tests, which meant he had to continue learning and studying; Angela had, after all, saved him only the embarrassment of recital. So it wasn't so bad, was it? Well, of course it was. As a child he had spent enough Wednesday afternoons in catechism to spot the velvet ripples of casuistry he was riding on now. But he didn't have the energy to care. His mind had more poisonous fish to fry. *Suppose* . . .

In addition to Greek, the Symposium and Herman Howell's course, Artie was also taking a seminar in bibliography given by the friendly director of the Houghton Library, who each Wednesday between three and five would show students treasures ranging from twelfth-century Syriac manuscripts on vellum to forged Shakespeare folios to first editions of Jane Austen, with time out at four for tea and cookies baked by his daughter-in-law. Assignments in the course were few, easy and generally interesting; and after Greek, Artie proceeded from Cleaver to the archaic world of the Houghton in order to do the latest of them: a descriptive report on a late-seventeenth-century English prayer book.

It was a shame that the assignments had to be done in what was undoubtedly the worst place at Harvard for Artie to be these days. To sit in the Houghton's reading room was to imagine the ravishing of quartos, the rape of octavos, the pulverizing of duodecimos. When he worked in here last week, he had posed to himself numerous hypotheses on the order of *Suppose I just ripped up that Herbert manuscript*, and he knew that he had been getting worse ever since.

In the fall of 1973 the reading room's extreme quiet was somewhat disturbed by noise from the construction of the underground Pusey Library, but otherwise a ferocious decorum continued to maintain itself. One checked one's coat and book bag outside, and even then could pass through the hobnailed leather door only after a librarian pushed a buzzer and released a lock. After that, one waited at a polished wooden table for an attendant to bring one's requested rarities. Once they arrived, one worked under the fierce eye of the elderly German woman (with an astonishingly protruding posterior), who presided over the room from the main desk, and who generally eyed the patrons as if they had a mind to walk away with the place.

As Artie waited, hands in pockets, for the prayer book to be brought, his eyes darted from one object to another: the huge glass-and-gold clock behind which he could see the librarians' offices, the oil portraits above the shelves of catalogues, the typewriters equipped with silencers alongside some of the tables. Books could be hurled at the portraits, typewriters flung through the clock. By the time the attendant arrived, Artie was so tired that he didn't see how he could complete the simple assignment ahead of him. With quivering hands he measured the cover of the book with a ruler and noted his finding on a yellow pad. He then moved to open the book itself.

He was interrupted by the fast and angry crepe-soled steps of the huge-bottomed librarian bearing down on him. *What have I done?* Artie wondered, his eyes careening from the clock to the portraits to the bookshelves. Had it finally happened? Had he actually done something horrible?

The librarian grabbed his wrist. "Here vee use zee pencil, not zee pen, my dear." She confiscated the Bic Artie had forgetfully fished from his pocket and slapped a freshly sharpened number

2 pencil into his hand, retreating on her crepe soles as swiftly as she had approached.

Artie was still nodding thank you after she had reached her desk.

Assistant Professor Jeffrey Stanhope, whom Artie had not noticed, saw what had happened and took Artie's apparent discomfort for merely boyish, if somewhat exaggerated, distress over having pulled an academic boner. He watched him fighting to regain the wherewithal to get on with his assignment, and he smiled.

Artie did not see his benevolent expression. As he copied out the title page with the pencil he'd been given, he was trying to figure out whether the sound he heard coming from the Pusey site was a mechanical saw or a police siren.

"Jesus H. Some place, Angela," Elizabeth marveled.

"Thank you, love. Come in and sit down. Arthur is already here." He had arrived ten minutes before, looking chalky, having skipped lunch and put in as many hours in Widener as his nerves could manage. Angela had appraised his appearance and shaken her head. "We'll deal with you later," she'd said, propelling him toward a Chesterfield sofa and returning to the kitchen to make choice little sandwiches.

Elizabeth also seemed impatient with his wretchedness. "You look like hell," she offered, sitting down on a mahogany chair across from the sofa. "What gives?"

"It's sort of a long story," Artie said.

Elizabeth nodded. "It figures. Everything around this place is. Hey, Angela, come in and sit down. You're paying the rent."

"I'm on my way, dear," Angela sang, returning to the living room with a tray full of drinks. Artie could tell that his looks and manner were making both women jumpy and that they were glad of each other's company. Where Angela was concerned, he was still lucid enough to surmise, this solidarity was something of an emotional exception. She might like Elizabeth's unstylish bluntness, but Artie could tell she was inclined to view most women, in an outmoded way, as competitors rather than "sisters." He had heard her refer with special contempt to some of the "females" in the Symposium. But for the moment she and Elizabeth seemed at one in warding off his weirdness.

"So," Angela said, settling herself, "what has your day been like?"

"Don't ask," Elizabeth answered, dragging on her Camel. "I just came from Blankman's seminar."

"Oh, you mean the little furry one?" Angela inquired.

"That's the one. I'm telling you, this guy is so berserk he makes Canker and the rest of them look like they could be Leave It to Beaver's father. After he got tenure, he somehow got into structuralism and all the other with-it jazz that's such a no-no here. So he's an embattled prophet now, kinda like one of these sandwich-sign crazies in the Square. Today he was talking about 'Young Goodman Brown' and the 'deep structure' and, I don't know, the subdural hematomas of each paragraph. Between every two sentences he inhales like a kettle in reverse and lets out this little cackle. It's gross."

Angela tsked in sympathy.

"And I'm sitting next to the one who wears so much blush-on she looks like she's got welts—"

"Oh, you mean Miss Enthusiasm," Angela said.

"You got her," Elizabeth continued. "Every so often she starts cooing like a loon about how '*won*derful it is to read such a tale on a *win*dy night by an *o*pen casement.' 'Casement,' do you believe it? The rest of us got windows. This chick's got casements. I thought I was gonna pass out."

"Why, were you loaded?" Richard Marbury affably inquired through the apartment door that Angela had left open.

"Richard, darling. Come in!"

"Hi, everybody."

"So where the hell were you during Blankman's seminar?" Elizabeth asked.

"I overslept."

"Swell, Richard. Maybe he should start at four instead of three. Actually, better he shouldn't start at all. You missed total squat."

"I figured," said Richard, who would not have been alarmed in any case. "So, Little Nell Trilling was there?" he asked Elizabeth, using their name for the blush-on girl from Bard and imitating her birdy flutings.

"In all her glory," Elizabeth replied.

"I think she has a crush on Artie," Richard announced. "A few days ago she referred to you as 'the boy in Symposium with the *won*derfully thin and sensitive hands.' She asked me if I knew what you wanted to do your thesis on."

"Well, sweetie! Here comes love!" Angela said.

"Oh, my God," said Artie. "Now *I'm* going to pass out."

Actually, he almost was, having consumed fewer than eight hundred calories in the last forty-eight hours. But even when Richard pronounced, "Hey, Angela, these are orgasmic," after eating a handful of sandwiches and cookies, Artie still didn't have the stomach for any food. He resumed his silent sweating. Angela glared at him; Elizabeth kept smoking; Richard kept eating. "God, I really shouldn't be scarfing these things up like such a pig," he said. "I'm supposed to play squash tonight."

"Nonsense," said Angela. "Scarf away. You poor boy. You must be sick of the fodder in that penal dining room near the dormitories. I'll bet you haven't had a decent dinner in weeks. When we're finished here we're all going straight over to the Blue Parrot for some spaghetti. My treat. No arguments now."

"Great," said Richard, who was unaccustomed to arguing about anything.

Angela was now firmly in command of the group and chose this moment to propose her first scheme—that the four of them divide up the reading list for the master's examinations and share their notes. Angela would take two of the five periods, medieval and Renaissance, because she could already quote nearly every line of each assigned text from memory. Richard was to handle the eighteenth century, Elizabeth the nineteenth and twentieth. (At Harvard all literature since 1800 was considered to fall into a single period of recent developments.) "And Arthur will do the awful American for us all," Angela explained, "since he's already embarked upon constructing a deluxe special edition for me. The two of us struck another deal in addition to this one, but there's no need to go into that. I suspect you'll get something a bit less comprehensive and grand from him, but I'm sure it will be perfectly adequate. Well, are we in agreement? After all, it only makes good sense. The law students do this all the time. It prepares them for a prosperous life of collusion. There's no reason we should have to be so solitary and slavish about everything. After all, when Chaucer said, 'gladly wolde he lerne, and gladly teche,' he couldn't have known that one day such enterprises would involve Ernest Hemingway and Lewis Sinclair."

They were agreed. Artie could not have opposed anything in his present state (and he was getting the best share of the bargain); Richard was constitutionally agreeable; and Elizabeth knew a good deal when she saw one.

"Lovely," said Angela. "I do have some slightly more subversive proposals to put to you, but we'll let them wait until dinner. Meanwhile, one more round?"

As they celebrated this first pact, gossip about life in Warble House gave way to revelations of the particular paths that had led each of them to graduate school and Harvard.

For Richard it had been a matter of accident as well as disinclination toward thinking about a career. He liked reading and while at Amherst had written well and without much effort about literature. His former girlfriend, unbeknownst to him, had procured an application to the Harvard English department. She filled it out for him and he signed it. Accepted some months later, he showed up during the second week of classes.

For Elizabeth it was more a matter of destiny and coercion:

"Everybody on both sides of the family, from Germany and Austria, has been in the academic racket since Hamlet was at Wittenberg. When it got to be refugee time, they all went the CCNY route—you know, Schopenhauer and schnitzel on the IRT. 'And now vere vill you go to schkool, Elizabeth? And vot vill you shtudy?' This was at age eleven. I told them I wanted to be one of the Ronettes, which was not considered an answer. Eventually I made it into Smith and Radcliffe and decided to go to NYU. I considered this mildly rebellious. My mother says it's what killed my father. I'm here now 'cause every Chanukah at home seems like Inquisition time—to mix your religious holidays and metaphors. I couldn't take the guilt anymore. I still like books, actually, although this place is doing its best to kill that off. So what's your story, Downing? Hand me one of those chocolate things first."

Angela's story was that after her divorce from Anthony Harley she had found herself "spitlessly bored" in a huge flat in Knightsbridge.

"Even better than this place?" Richard asked.

"Darling, I don't mean to put on *le chien*, but this place looks rather like an *abattoir* in comparison."

"Jesus," Elizabeth said, shaking her head. "Gimme another chocolate ball."

Angela explained that after the divorce she had resumed an affair with a Cambridge don who was "rather stupid but rather sweet" and who had advised her to do a further degree. "Well, I was bored, and I did have occasion to read the silly little academic effusions he was turning out himself, and I thought, oh, well, really, if someone is going to have to write these things, it might as well be someone who'll write them splendidly. So I decided it should be myself. And since I was bored, I thought I'd try America to boot."

"Even though you hate the literature," Richard reminded her.

"Despise it, sweetie. But absolutely *love* the television. In fact, we should probably be moving on to the Blue Parrot. I don't want to be home too late for *Hawaii Five-O.*"

They made moves to drink up, but were all startled into immobility when Artie, giddy with hunger and fatigue, began, for the first time since he'd responded to news of the blush-on girl's crush, to speak—in the kind of word-rush he was accustomed to spilling into Shane's sleeve: "I'm sort of supposed to be the last step in Irish upward mobility. I mean, that's how it would look to a lot of people, why I'm here, I mean. Nobody knows what my great-great-grandfather did in Ireland before the famine, but they sort of suspect it wasn't completely on the level, and then the family came over here and my great-grandfather worked in a saloon on Tenth Avenue and my grandfather was a doorman at the Statler and my father is, you know, white collar—he works in an accounts department on Fifth Avenue—and so it looks like I'm the next logical step. You know, entering the professions and all that. I mean, I'm the first person in my family ever to go to college, much less graduate school. But I really didn't come here to, you know, go up in the world. I came here because I really love literature. I mean, I don't want to sound like Little Nell, but I really do. I still remember the first time I read 'Ode to a Nightingale.' I was in college, I was a freshman; I hadn't gone to a really good high school—I mean, I'd *heard* of Keats, but we never actually read him—and, well, when I read that poem I knew I wanted to keep reading for the rest of my life. And that's why I came here. I mean, I think I thought it offered the best chance for me to keep doing that. But in the last two months I've gotten sort of confused, not just about this place, but really, sort of, about myself, and, actually, now, I, well, I really don't know . . . why . . . I'm here."

He subsided into blankness. Elizabeth and Richard looked at each other in alarm. Angela, taking charge, said in her customary lilt, "Let's see. Richard, the car keys are on the little table near the door. Perhaps you and Elizabeth could go out and warm it up—it's the little BMW just by the corner. Arthur and I will come down and join you in just a second."

As soon as Elizabeth and Richard were gone, Artie said, "Oh, Angela, I'm sorry. I've been—"

"I know. Crazy. It shows, sweetie. Now listen to me. This is rather an awkward moment for dry sobs and nervous collapse and that sort of thing. After all, we don't want our little circle to fall apart just as it's getting off to such a nice start. So, let's do this: you take yourself in hand and put off this breakdown until, oh, about eleven. In the meantime, you come with us and try to be cheery. Then, back here, after *Hawaii Five-O,* you can go nicely to pieces and I'll pick them right up. All right? At the moment there's little else you can do. And besides, it's imperative that you gorge yourself with some pasta. You look positively Biafran, and for the last hour you've eaten nothing but your napkin, an ingestion which I've found rather disgusting, but which I've been keeping my eye on nonetheless. Now come, love, do as I say. The motor's running."

"I just sort of zip around until I find what it is I'm looking for," Angela said, explaining why she was driving too fast down Mass. Ave. in the direction away from the Blue Parrot.

"That's a good idea," Richard said agreeably.

"Angela," protested Elizabeth. "We're gonna be eating in Dorchester if you keep this up. Look, we're back in the Square and you're still headed in the wrong direction."

"Oh, dear," said Angela, without a hint of changing course.

Suppose I just grabbed the wheel and sent us all flying up onto the sidewalk, right into those people . . .

They had to stop at a light.

"Excuse me, please," said Artie. "I don't think I'm going to be able to make it tonight. I've got to go." He opened the door next to the death seat, and before Angela could reach over to restrain him he left the car. She shouted after him, but the light turned green and the Boston driver behind her was using his horn.

It was the sight of Holyoke Center that made him bolt the car. This, he knew, walking through the center's arcade, hands in pockets and eyes on feet, was the moment he had to act. He might not make it through another hour.

He entered the main part of the building, stepped into the elevator and hit the button for the third floor. In ten seconds he was in front of a desk marked "Reception—University Health Services" and talking to a nurse.

"Yeah?" she asked, after he gave her his bursar's card.

"Psych—" Artie stammered, his mouth dry.

"Sick?" she asked, hearing Artie's stress-induced New York pronunciation. "Well, you came to the right place. What's the matter?"

"Psych—i—" Artie stumbled.

"Sick eye? You want the ophthalmologist?"

"Psychiatrist," Artie finally managed to say.

"Oh, the head shrinkers. They're up on the sixth floor. But it's six-thirty, honey. They've all gone home. I'll give you an appointment. Tomorrow afternoon, okay? I'll set you up with Mrs. Crangel. She's a peach. Come in at four-thirty."

7

How could she be *smiling*? Her eyes showed intelligence and sympathy, so how could she smile after listening to his breathless recital about the demons, which had ended: "And then I knew I couldn't stand it anymore, and so I jumped out of the car and came here for an appointment . . . My God, I don't believe I'm really telling you all this."

"Arthur, I'm not going to drop a net over you." Her smile turned into a giggle. "That's what you're afraid of, isn't it?"

"You mean that somebody is going to lock me up? Nobody can really do that, can they?"

"No. You don't need to be in a hospital. Perhaps you'd like to be, though?"

"No, I wouldn't!" Artie responded. "Why should I?"

Mrs. Crangel shrugged. "Well, you wouldn't have to make any decisions, wouldn't have any streets to cross, wouldn't have to be thinking about windows and bricks all the time. It could be nice. In fact, it would be a little like living in one big pocket."

Artie withdrew his hands from his jeans. A few moments ago his body had been shaking; now it marshaled all its neurological ebullitions into a blush. Was the whole world bent on teasing him? Would Mrs. Crangel be like Angela and Shane, who tried to soothe with verbal tweaking? He had heard of the decade's new therapies, like primal scream; was Mrs. Crangel an exponent of the primal tickle? He turned his blushing face up from his lap and toward her. She was tall and angular—"lanky" was probably the word he was looking for—and she sprawled more than sat in one of the Health Services' modern chairs, the kind that look like dessert cups on legs. She was comfortable inside her own skin. She was about forty, had big eyes and big teeth and thick brown hair that she hanked behind her ears. Her eyes were bordered by what cosmetologists would call, accurately in her case, "laugh lines." She had a little of West Texas left in her voice, and the overall effect of her sound and carriage made Artie imagine her, after the last appointment of the day, making a quick change into a pair of straight-legged jeans, hopping on a horse tethered in the parking lot and cantering home up Brattle Street. He was certain, though there were no pictures on her desk or office walls, that she had children at home and that they were crazy about her. He tended to make up his mind about people all at once, and he liked her immensely. But did she have to smile at what he'd just told her? He could understand how his demons might sound funny, and maybe she was trying to put him at ease, but something in him was hurt by the way she seemed to belittle the sweaty frights he'd been having for two weeks.

Then, as if she could read his mind (a capacity that, he would later reflect, was her business), she broke the silence in the small white office by saying, "Arthur, I don't mean to minimize what you've been feeling. But you must know that these—whatever you want to call them—'episodes' are just signs of other things, don't you?"

Artie looked at her intently. "What's wrong with me?" he asked.

Once again, to both his comfort and dismay, she smiled. "Well, that's what we've got to find out."

"Does anything occur to you right away?" Artie asked, hoping for an analytical panacea but asking the question in an offhand way, so as to indicate he wouldn't consider her guilty of malpractice if she just hazarded a guess.

"Going out on a limb," she answered, "I would say there's both a good deal more and a good deal less wrong with you than you think."

"Tell me about the less part," Artie requested.

"Well, these 'episodes'—I don't think they mean very much in themselves. I'll bet you they go away as suddenly as they came."

"Really?" asked Artie, hopeful and energized. "How? Why? What do you call them, anyway?"

She took his stream of questions in stride. "I could apply names to them, but I'm not sure how accurate or helpful they'd be. But if you like. You mentioned you're taking Greek. You can figure out the word 'agoraphobia,' can't you?"

Artie did not need Angela for this one. "But that's when you're afraid to go out of your house, isn't it? When you're afraid of crowds?"

"Well, you haven't exactly felt like going to Fenway Park most afternoons, have you?"

"But doesn't agoraphobia mean you think something terrible's going to happen to you? I keep worrying about *doing* something terrible."

"Doesn't it amount to the same thing? You're going to do something terrible—something you have no desire to do—and then you're going to be terribly punished. Look, if I wanted to, I could tell you it sounds to me like you've got some sort of 'obsessive-compulsive reverse agoraphobia' "—her pronunciation mocked the words' grandiosity—"but I don't want to."

"Why not?" Artie asked.

"Because a lot of words aren't very helpful. Sometimes what's in all those books is useful," she said, pointing to her shelves of texts and journals, "and sometimes it's not. Maybe in your case names and definitions aren't."

"Then how will I know what I've got?" Artie asked, once again discouraged.

"Maybe you haven't 'got' anything," Mrs. Crangel offered.

Artie looked at her, bewildered.

"This is the 'more' part. Maybe all these nightmare questions—*suppose* this, *suppose* that—are really just scary little substitutes for big questions, real ones, that you're afraid to ask."

"Like what?" Artie asked, intrigued.

"Oh, like what do you want to do with your life, who do you want to fall in love with, who do you think you are, what do you think the world is about."

"This sounds more like philosophy than psychology."

"Sometimes all psychology is is practical philosophy."

"You mean like applied mathematics?"

"Something like that. The point is that as long as you keep worrying about throwing library books down sewers, you don't have to ask those big questions, do you?"

"You mean I'm deliberately putting myself through all this? So I can avoid what's *really* bothering me?"

"You may be. I think we can find that out. And I think we can find out why you're so frightened of losing control. Control of what? Let's try to find that out, too."

"So you think you can work with me?"

"I'm afraid, Arthur, that it's my professional duty to tell you that you are not beyond hope. And that furthermore you are condemned to go on living life—and maybe, God forbid, enjoying some of it—while you try to straighten these things out. So why don't you come see me this time next week and we'll see what we can come up with. In the meantime, I'm going to give you a couple of prescriptions for things that will make you feel better." She handed him two pieces of note paper. "See you next week," she said.

Artie was silenced by the speed with which things seemed to be moving. Mrs. Crangel smiled. "You look as if you're waiting for me to assign your penance. Sorry. No Our Fathers and no Hail Marys. Just come in next week at four-thirty. Okay?"

"Okay," Artie responded. "And thank you," he added. A gulp of emotion came up in him as he shook her hand. "Thank you very much, Dr. Crangel."

"Arthur, I'm not a doctor. I'm a psychiatric social worker. I can write prescriptions because everything here is supervised by the bona fide shrinks."

"Oh," said Artie.

"And you can call me Diana."

Artie looked uncomfortable.

"Oh, lord." She laughed. "If that's too much of a breakthrough for you to handle all at once, 'Mrs. Crangel' will do. So long, hon."

As Artie walked toward the elevator, he kept his eyes on his shoes, not because he was afraid of visiting calamities upon the receptionist and waiting patients, but because he didn't like the thought of being seen here. He tapped the little white call button for the elevator several times more than was necessary.

When it arrived and the door opened, he saw Assistant Professor Jeffrey Stanhope step out and greet him.

"Hello. Artie Dunne, right?"

"Yes. How are you?"

"Fine. How did that work in the Houghton go the other day?"

Had he been there? Had he seen him reprimanded by the great-bottomed keeper of the reading room?

"Oh, it was fine. It was pretty easy, actually. You know. Bibliographical description."

"That's good," Jeffrey said. "How's everything otherwise?"

"Oh, fine," said Artie, rubbing his jaw in a burst of inspiration. "Except for my tooth. I just had my tooth filled. It hurts a little. My tooth."

"Oh, sorry about that," Jeffrey replied. "I thought the dentists were way up near the top floor. I come to see a psychiatrist each week on this one."

"Oh. Right," said Artie.

Jeffrey smiled down at him. "In fact, I'm a little late for him right now. Listen, why don't we have dinner sometime? Give me a call."

"Okay," said Artie, embarrassed and surprised.

"Good," said Jeffrey. "I'll talk to you." He patted Artie's shoulder and went off, tall and handsome, down the hall.

Walking across the Square to a pharmacy, Artie was beset with the usual number of "supposes." But he was trying to fight them off now—after all, weren't they just signs of other, very normal, problems? He was determined not to lose the little shock of optimism he had received in Mrs. Crangel's office. Inside the drug store he gave the pharmacist the prescriptions. A few minutes later he was handed a small vial labeled "Valium, 5 mg." as well as one of Mrs. Crangel's two pieces of paper.

"I can't fill this," the pharmacist said.

Artie looked at the note. "Two cheeseburgers. Large French fries. One milk shake."

With the lifelong inclination to obey authority that Angela found so exasperating, Artie went up Mass. Ave. to Charlie's Beef and Beer and complied exactly with Mrs. Crangel's second prescription. Mouthful by mouthful, amid the dark fake wood paneling and unseasonable air conditioning, he managed to work his way through the whole order. He was relieved to find himself first hungry and then bloated. It was beginning to look as if, whatever other assault strategies they might have in store, the demons would not succeed in starving him into submission. He dared to hope, as he half burped and half hiccuped, that things might be looking up. Had he been Shane, he thought, he would have belched for the full auditory benefit of his fellow diners; being who he was, he allowed his esophagus to make no more than a demure confidence into his napkin. He paid his bill and left.

It was just past seven but quite black with October night. The air was clean and brisk, and for the first time in weeks Artie felt more like being outdoors than in. He could, if he wanted, get back to the Comus lounge in time to catch Eric Sevareid's comment on the latest battle surrounding the White House tapes, but he didn't want to. He would rather breathe in some of the night. So he went to the Cambridge Common and sat on a bench.

His walk there was not particularly easy: his hands remained in his pockets and his eyes hugged the ground. Plenty of store windows along the route looked vulnerable; garbage cans were as kickable as ever. But it had been a good afternoon, and Artie wasn't going to lose the feeling he had left Mrs. Crangel's with — namely, that the demons might begin to shrink; that they might be captured in a box that had to be opened only one hour each week; that they might in the end be exposed, like a practical joke, for the worthwhile quandaries of which they were symptoms.

On the Common one found people who actually lived, not just matriculated, in Cambridge. It was an exotic place to Artie's suburban spirit. Within a fifty-foot radius of his bench he could hear an old Trotskyite argue about the Yom Kippur War with a red-bearded New Leftist, now that it was too dark for the two of them to keep playing chess; listen to two blue-coated lesbians exchange tips on the cooking of paella and gossip about the Rape Crisis Center, as they kept their eyes on their young sons cavorting over the Revolutionary War cannon; and observe, just beyond them, a junior high school girl selling marijuana to a high school boy. It was a tranquil night in the commonwealth, for all the uncertainty in the larger republic. The trolley cables clicked and whizzed, and the stars came out over the university and its poorer neighbors.

Besides Greek, all Artie had tomorrow was the bibliography seminar. It would be an easy day, and he did not want to work tonight. He wanted to celebrate what he hoped was a turning point. He would not go back to Comus to read. He would go see Angela.

He felt guilty about her. He hadn't seen her since bolting her car. Last night and today she had called the third floor in Comus and left messages, but he had been too preoccupied to call back. All he'd been able to do was wait for his appointment with Mrs.

Crangel. Maybe she was really anxious about him. He decided, however many "supposes" he had to endure, however much hand-pocketing and pedi-vision he had to suffer, that he would walk all the way to the river and her apartment.

When he buzzed from the lobby, Angela released the door right away, without calling down to find out who it was—surely a sign of worry. He quickly mounted the stairs. He knocked at the door.

"It's open," she called.

He found her lying on the Chesterfield sofa with some white wine in a glass the size of a brandy snifter. On her lap was volume three of J. M. French's *Life Records of John Milton*, but she wasn't paying attention to it. She was watching *Medical Center*.

"Well, as I live and breathe," she said in a tone Artie understood to indicate mild relief and slightly warmer exasperation. "It's Oliver Twist come back at last. Well, sit down, sweetie. But not a word. This is reaching a very critical moment. The little girl on the screen has a diseased kidney or fibula or something, and her younger sister is going to donate whatever it is that she needs. She's the only one who can do it because she's got the same blood type or eye color or some such thing. The doctor over there with those marvelously pretty ears—I *do* fancy ears, don't you?—is trying to put everyone at their ease, but he's being distracted by this wretched man down the hall who keeps muttering about malpractice because some tiny error's been made that's cost him his sight. Here, darling, have some wine and keep still."

Artie had no choice but to comply until the girl who needed a kidney (it was a kidney, not a fibula) underwent a successful transplant and the man down the hall miraculously regained the use of his eyes. "Oh, goodie," Angela exclaimed. "I do so like happy endings, don't you?" She lowered the volume on the set.

"Uh-huh," answered Artie. "What's the Milton book for?" he

asked, disappointed at Angela's lack of anxiety and unsure how to make conversation.

"The commercials. It's really rather boring, though, when one knows the story. You know, the civil war, the blindness, the epics. Pity he couldn't have seen handsome Dr. Gannon about the old eyes. Well, love, what about your own neurasthenia, or whatever I should call it?"

"You mean why I was so nervous yesterday?"

" 'Nervous'? That's rather like saying a cat has been observed to be furry. I thought you were about to decompose all over the carpet," she said, rubbing a bare toe into a bit of Oriental fiber. "Now where did you go after you jumped from my car? Really, it was rather breathtaking, like something on *Hawaii Five-O*."

"I had," said Artie, once more embarrassed, "to go see a doctor."

"Some sort of psychotherapist, I suppose? Well, perhaps you won't look so dreadfully like someone strapped to a paint mixer now. Does it appear as if it's going to do any good?"

"Oh, yes, Angela! I saw this woman named Crangel, and I think she's wonderful. After just an hour she seemed to know exactly how to start handling whatever's bothering me. She's terrific. I already feel so grateful to her."

"Well," said Angela, intrasexual jealousy putting a bit of a chill into her voice, "of course it's all verbal placebo pretending to be medicine, but as long as it helps. I suppose that's what's important."

Artie felt the wind leave his new therapeutic sails. His lower lip protruded slightly, until Angela, apparently over her reflexive rivalry, warmed up and smiled. "Now, love, I don't suppose you'd like to tell *me* just what's been making you so febrile?"

"It's kind of hard," Artie answered.

"I suppose it is. Well, we'll just let the female head healer take care of it, then. Let me tell you about our little gathering at the Blue Parrot. Incidentally, Elizabeth and Richard have been quite worried about you, as have I. We've all been calling that awful place you live and this lispy little boy keeps taking messages, which I fear he's not delivering, or which you, in your agitated melancholy, are ignoring. In any case, for all our distress over you we did manage to dine together and *guess* who should be not three tables away from us?"

"Who?" asked Artie.

"Damon and Piteous themselves. That's right, Branded and Canker. Fervently discussing some little tributary of neoclassicism, as well, no doubt, as the appalling quality of mind of the young protégé's fellow students, i.e., ourselves."

"Oh, no," said Artie.

"Oh, yes. They were blissfully content with one another. I thought for a moment Canker might feed Branded a bit of spaghetti from his fork, like a mama bird bestowing a choice worm upon the favorite of her young. It was really rather ghastly."

"God," said Artie.

"Well, it wasn't *so* bad, in one sense. It did propel us to certain subversive depths that we might otherwise have failed to reach. We've concocted one or two plans to, shall we say, clear the air in Warble House. The first of them is to go into effect two weeks from Friday, when Canker holds the Symposium in the Houghton Reading Room so that we can discuss Dryden's literary 'remains.' God, I suppose it *takes* remains to *know* remains. But that's beside the point. We have a little surprise planned. If we don't get the chance to fill you in between now and then, you'll just have to remain a bit in the dark—rather like those poor Cuban men at the Watergate—but don't worry, we'll take care of you. Incidentally, I do wish they would stop hounding that troubled man," she said, pointing to the television, which was, at the beginning of a special broadcast, transmitting the face of Richard Nixon to the American public.

"You mean Nixon!" Artie cried.

"Of course I mean Nixon," Angela replied. "This unfortunate man has just succeeded in stealing that lovely house in California, and these awful liberals aren't going to let him enjoy it for a moment." Angela, whose rebelliousness did not extend to matters concerning the world economy or general order, uttered the word "liberal" more as if it were something she was being forced to smell than speak. The one time she and Artie had exchanged a few words about politics, several days before, she had expressed enthusiasm for a Conservative British politician he'd never heard of, someone named Thatcher. "She is, of course, a woman, but then so's Edward Heath," she had explained.

"Let's see, where were we?" she asked, shutting off the television. "Oh, yes, our group's little plans. Well, we're all going out to do a bit of drinking Friday night. Perhaps you can learn more then. We can count on you, can't we?"

"Oh, of course. What time?" Artie asked, actually alarmed by Angela's plans, but reasoning that with her as leader none of them could come to any harm.

"About nine. We'll meet here."

"Fine."

"Oh, good. Do have some more wine," she said, turning off one of the lights and refilling Artie's glass. "There. Now, love, are you sure you don't want to tell dear Angela any more about your troubles?"

Artie noticed that his hair was being stroked by her left hand, that his ribs were being explored by her right and that his ear was being breathed into. He realized what was happening and began to go giddy. This seemed a miracle on the order of the advent of Mrs. Crangel, and he couldn't take it all in. After the extreme nervousness of the morning, his preprandial Valium, the ensuing cheeseburgers and the wine, he felt wonderful about what Angela was initiating, but not quite able to follow through on it. Her exploration of his ribs became more of a tickle, and this physical stimulation, combined with his sudden surge of mental well-being, made him laugh hilariously. It was a minute or two before he could manage the breath to say, "Not tonight, please. I have a nervous breakdown." Then he began to laugh again, and for the first time in about two months his laughter was directed at least partially toward himself.

Angela, to his relief, laughed too. She ceased tickling him, gave a huge smile, kissed him on the nose and said, "All right, love. Friday, then. Without fail. Or else I'll break your little arm."

8

The next day Artie lost most of the optimism born in Mrs. Crangel's office and released at Angela's apartment. Greek class was beginning to seem more and more unreal as he depended on Angela's mysteriously remote translations; if he didn't begin to study on his own, he would never pass the final. When the bibliography seminar broke for the professor's daughter-in-law's refreshments, he was plagued by thoughts of illuminated manuscripts dunked in the tea, Gutenberg Bibles smeared with chocolate chips. The walk home was mined with as many "supposes" as ever. The only thing to cheer him as he arrived back in Comus, after dark, was his mail, which included a giant-sized postcard from Shane.

The postmark was Las Vegas. The picture was of a pie-eyed Shriner with G-strings dangling from his fez. The message was:

Urn Man:

Last night I won $38 and the attentions of a Dunkin' Donuts waitress. Neither one much of a windfall, but probably the last chips I'm gonna be in until I hit the Silicon Valley and Brother Bill. (Speaking of silicon: the D.D. chick was no stranger to it, I think.) If you remember geography—and you're such a goddamn smart little weenie, you will—you'll realize I'm taking the scenic route thither. Can't take it much longer, either. In no hurry to see the bro', but by now the car smells like Juniper and's got about as much energy as Boodie.

Well, JK, is your head any better than it was ere we last parted? At said time you looked like you'd just been getting the kiss-off from Fanny Brawne — or the news that the consumption test had come back +. Don't head for any Roman rest cures without letting
Shane
know.

Artie wondered whether Shane had by now arrived at his brother's and got the letter he'd mailed Saturday night. He tried to picture him coming home from work in a few hours (California time) and finding it. But for all he knew, Shane had decided at the last moment, despite the condition of the car, to make the last part of the journey via Guadalajara, or Vancouver.

It bothered him not to know where Shane was. Like Angela's translated sentences, it frustrated his sense of reality. Mrs. Crangel said psychology was just a branch of philosophy. If that was so, Artie felt he was up to the chapter on epistemology. How do we know what we know? How did Angela know what English words fit which Greek ones? How could he be sure of what he only surmised — that Shane still walked and talked somewhere, a continent away? He needed to see him, hear his voice. He needed his advice.

About Angela, for instance, Shane had been right. Far from wanting to kill him (though there was the threat to his arm to consider), she wanted to seduce him. In fact, she might as well have already. Friday night was a lay *accompli*; Artie could no more defy her than he could have a draft board officer or a nun. And he didn't want to. He'd dreamed about the weekend all morning in Widener.

But anticipation didn't mean Shane's advice was no longer required. Artie could think of a dozen questions to ask him about the mechanics, etiquette, implications and aftermath of what he and Angela were soon to do. Since there was no way of getting such advice, he decided he would try to forget about Angela tonight and get some work done. After a dinner of soup, he once more skipped the news in favor of sitting behind his desk, first with the religious poetry of Richard Crashaw, for Herman Howell's class, and then with his opaquely clarified Greek.

He did all right until 10:00, Crashaw's meditations and the vocative singular making occasional sense to him. But as he tired his brain drifted back toward Angela, the sight of a mere gamma or theta triggering thoughts of her. His mind went out to the corridor noises, too. About this hour things usually became more bizarrely audible, as if the Thorazine were wearing off the patients in the ward. An argument was going on. The Chinese physics student (the one who purged his sinuses each morning in the shower) was screaming, "I will *kill* you! I will *kill* you!" to a Spanish philosophy student. It seemed, Artie gathered through the impediments of volume and accent, that the Spanish philosophy student had broken into the Chinese physics student's room and seized over two thousand note cards pertaining to the latter's dissertation-in-progress on a tricky new aspect of quantum theory. He had then shuffled the unnumbered cards into a hopelessly impenetrable new order.

Though the Chinese physics student couldn't be brought to acknowledge it, this action had not been without cause. The Spanish philosophy student had undertaken his covert mission because the previous evening the Chinese physics student had, quite overtly, dumped the Spanish philosophy student's boiling pot of rice and tomatoes down one of the bathroom sinks. This action had also been more one of retaliation than provocation. The Chinese physics student had seized the pot of rice from the Spanish philosophy student's hot plate because of its tendency to extract flames from whatever outlet into which it was plugged; it was widely regarded as the reason the third-floor fuse had on Monday night blown out for the fourth time that month, setting off some anxious sobs from Voltears and plunging the residents into a darkness so literal that the study of quantum physics and all else became impossible until power was restored.

It appeared that tonight's crisis might go on for some time. As the Chinese physics student and the Spanish philosophy student continued their abuse, other residents of the third floor emerged from their rooms to observe and placate. The Hedgehog, whose problematic path had been blocked by the altercation, did a lot of reasoning with the disputing parties. His efforts produced a modicum of unity but not on any of the relevant issues. "Fucking wall banger!" the Chinese physics student shouted at his interference. "Stupid fruit of loom!" the Spanish philosophy student cried.

The others remained silent as the negotiations ruptured. Voltears went off to peer into the stairwell, and Artie contemplated one more nighttime walk to the Square. But then the Gainsborough boy swerved around the corner, calling out in great excitement, "Oh, Artie! Artie! That guy with the really sexy voice is on the phone! He told me to go get you. I said, 'What*ever* you *say*!' "

Artie pushed past the debaters and sprinted down the corridor to the phone.

"Shane!"

"Who the fuck was that? And what the fuck is going on in that place? It sounds like a rumble between some Puerto Ricans and the Vietcong."

"It's just an argument over some vegetables and note cards," Artie said, eager not to waste any minutes of this unexpected talk. "It was the Blue Boy on the phone. Remember him that morning in the bathroom? I mentioned him in my letter. Did you get my letter?"

"Yeah. I just got it now. I just walked in. I'm at Mild Bill's," Shane explained, alluding to his managerial brother. "Jesus," he continued, returning to the question of the Blue Boy, "that guy said to me, 'Oh, you sound just like Brando!' This was after I said hello."

"He's a little extravagant," Artie explained.

"Just a mite. He also says he's worried about you. 'Your little friend is looking very thin,' is how he put it. 'Aren't you taking care of him?' So what's the story, Urn Man—still fucked-up?"

Artie didn't really know how to answer, but after a second's hesitation he found himself, as he always did talking to Shane, on automatic pilot, the words coming as fast as breath. "Oh, I guess so. Well, yeah, I am. Shane, you wouldn't believe some of the stuff I'm going through. Not just all the junk I told you about, but really weird stuff. I keep imagining all these awful things, really crazy things, are going to happen and sometimes I get so carried away with them that I can hardly walk down a street, and even though I went to see this lady psychiatrist and she says I'll be all right, I don't really know, I'm starting to think I'm nuts, and now in the middle of all this Angela, you remember her, she's the English woman who wrote the screw-kill couplet, well, she and I have almost started to become sort of, well, involved, and I know she definitely expects—in fact, she's just about *demanded*—we *become* involved—that's supposed to happen Friday—and I don't know if I can handle it, and there's still all this work that's driving me crazy, and God, I wish you were here. I still don't know what's going on."

He ran out of breath. Shane paused a moment on the other end.

"Is that it? End of ode? Last stanza?" he asked.

"Sorry," Artie said. "I guess I'm really a little crazy, huh? Even more than usual?"

"JK, I think you've been afraid of going crazy since you were about twelve. You're so afraid of going nuts it's driving you nuts. When Roosevelt was talking all that nothing-to-fear-but-fear-itself jazz, he should have been talking to you instead of the Okies and the apple sellers. Nuts thou never wert."

It dimly registered in Artie's mind that this speech, while more idiomatic, was not so very different from Mrs. Crangel's remarks yesterday afternoon.

"I don't know, Shane. I feel nuts. I really do."

"Hey. Let not the merely fucked-up profane the travails of the truly nuts. That's in the Bible. You could look it up, as Casey Stengel used to say. You miss the Yankees, Urn Man? There you were, living in New York all those years as an urn kid, just a little bud vase, with the greatest team in the world right next door. And now all you've got are the piss-poor Red Sox. Did you ever think: what a falling-off was there?"

This seemed an unusually sharp change of subject, even for Shane. Artie couldn't help but ask, "Shane, are you on anything?"

"Just a little leftover herbal present from the chick at the Dunkin' Donuts. I ingested it in the employees' john this afternoon."

"Oh," said Artie.

"Look, JK," said Shane, taking charge and turning on the lucidity. "I'm a little *preoccupato* about you, as they used to say on Federal Hill. I want you to keep getting your ass to that shrink. And I want you to eat some goddamn food. I don't want any more alarming bulletins from the Brando fan, you hear me?"

"Okay," said Artie.

"And remember. You're fucked-up. Not nuts. So stay that way."

"Okay," said Artie. "But I don't see how I'm going to make it sometimes." He paused. "I wish I could see you."

"You will. June twenty-eight, nineteen seventy-four."

"Really?" asked Artie, amazed at the definiteness of the date, if appalled by its distance. "Why? How?"

"Mild Bill's getting wed to the Junior Leaguer of his dreams the following day—a Saturday—in Connecticut. I get to fly home *gratis*, thanks to the forebears. So. I'll see you the preceding Friday."

"Where? When?"

"What is this? A quiz?" Shane responded. "Okay. Remember that time we tooled down to New York and wound up wandering around the Frick, where I couldn't help but make the occasionally tasteless malapropism with the owner's name? Meet me under Saint Jerome's beard—you know, the El Greco job near the fireplace. Eleven o'clock."

"Okay," said Artie, trying to memorize the information, whispering it twice to make sure he had it straight.

"Urn Man?"

"Yeah?"

"I do think there will be time to confirm all this in writing."

"Will you?" Artie asked.

"Several times over. At the moment, I've got to get my butt into the dining room and set the table. Around here you can't even open a Bud without having to pour it into a goddamned glass. Anyway, keep your little nightingale's beak up. And eat some fuckin' pizza. So long, Keatslet. Happy Halloween."

By the time Artie said good-bye, Shane was off the line. "June twenty-eighth," Artie repeated to himself as he walked back to his room. "June twenty-eighth. I'll just keep thinking about June twenty-eighth."

He reached his door. "Franco fascist!" the Chinese physics student yelled to the Spanish philosophy student.

The Moon for the Misbegotten bar stood on a corner of Mass. Ave. halfway between Harvard and Central squares, which is to say halfway between the university and the "real" world of wage earners and early risers. It was a halfway place in spirit, too. Harvard graduate students were part of its clientele, but so were neighborhood working people, burned-out hippies, sometime artists. It was an Irish place, aggressively so. Snatches of Joyce and Yeats wafted through its smoky, boozy air along with unpleasant remarks about things and beings British. In the fall of 1973 rock was giving way to the first brutish pulsations of disco, but in the Moon one still heard fiddles and pipes.

On Friday night, as on most others, it was full to bursting, or, more precisely, breakage. It was common to see glasses fly as the night wore on, though often the Moon's large and psychologically astute bouncers were able to intercept them before they reached the mirrors.

Artie and his friends were seated around a small table in the back. The Moon was not a place in which patrons could easily hear one another, and for stretches of the two hours they were here, the four of them had to be content with smiling at each other instead of talking. These cacophonous silences gave Artie the chance to look at Angela and discover that she was tossing him the same expressions she had during Herman Howell's seminar yesterday afternoon: looks that were sensual, toothsome, brazenly anticipatory. Artie had to worry; this kind of humorous calculation made the possibility of genuine excitement on her part seem unlikely to him.

"Well, darling, I've tarted myself up just for you," she'd shouted to him when they entered the din. This particular feat of tarting had involved several hundred dollars' worth of gorgeously understated silk and wool. They all drank beer, except for her. She asked the bartender for a vodka-and-vodka ("a little invention of mine"). They all smoked except for Richard, who had just come from a squash game and was feeling limber. When the tide of noise went out for a minute, they managed a discussion of Elizabeth's tenancy troubles.

"I threatened to mail him a roach a day until he sends up some heat. Last night I froze my tush off. I was sitting in the kitchen reading Melville and wishing for a little more blubber of my own." The others shook their heads, commiserating. "You know, Angela," Elizabeth resumed, "Melville's not such New World schlock as you might think. You ought to try *Moby-Dick* sometime between hits of *The Faerie Queene.*"

"Oh, darling, all that sperm and all those prostheses?"

"You can skip a lot of the technical chapters, the stuff on whaling," Richard suggested. "Actually, it's sort of an allegory. The whale is kind of like God."

Angela, unconvinced, quoted Polonius: "Then God, sweetie, must be 'very like a whale.' Heavens, let's change the subject to more practical matters. How are you all doing with your periods?"

Richard, uncharacteristically disconcerted, seemed to be wondering whether Angela was speaking of punctuation or gynecology. He asked, "What periods?"

"The reading list, darling. Remember? We divided it up Monday. Really, Richard, no one admires your insouciance more than myself, but perhaps we need to tape a few little reminders to you every so often?"

"Oh," said Richard, smiling. "Those periods. I have the nineteenth century, right?"

"No, love, the eighteenth."

"Jesus, Angela," intervened Elizabeth. "It's only been four days since we chopped it up. Who's got time to think about it? It's all I can do to get ready for Blankman's seminar Monday. I just know the chick with the blush-on is gonna talk about how '*thrill*ingly manly and inspi*ra*tional' the deckhands on the *Pequod* are."

"You're right, love," Angela conceded. "I suppose it is a bit early. It's just that I don't find myself terribly engaged by the classes just now. Even dear sweet Howell's. I must say, though, that it seems a different matter for our Arthur here," she said, tickling his forearm. "What a lovely little report he gave on Crashaw yesterday. The only Catholic poet on the list. I suppose that's why you volunteered to do him, isn't it, love? After all, you're still rather an R.C. yourself, aren't you?"

"Sort of," answered Artie.

"Sort of," repeated Angela, mimicking the monosyllabic tentativeness he constantly displayed in her presence. "Really, darling, I was hoping for a somewhat more theologically complex answer. What about the details? You're such a great believer in details, after all. Do you believe it *all?* Immaculate conception and the lot of it?"

"Well, it's possible," Artie answered.

"Really? A woman and a bird? Surely the Emperor's Society for the Prevention of Cruelty to Animals would have intervened? Oh, come, love, virgin birth indeed. Surely a virgin *dearth* was more likely the case in Galilee. Rather a warm place—they were all quite randy, I'm sure. And I'm equally sure they all did something about it at an early age."

Artie blushed.

"What about you, love?" she inquired of Elizabeth. "Are you a believer? Even a bit?"

"If lighting the candles counts as a bit, then I'm a bit," Elizabeth explained. "So's the whole family. But theology-wise their hearts really belong to Goethe, not Daddy," she elaborated, pointing toward the ceiling. "You know: love and literature will spread enlightenment all over the world. If Artie's Roman Catholic, they're Romantic Jewish. Humanists till it hurts. And boy, has it hurt."

Angela, sensing the conversation might be moving in the last direction she ever wished to go—namely, seriousness—turned to Richard. "And you, love?"

"Oh, me," Richard said, emerging from a haze. "Do I believe? Oh, I don't think so. I've never given it much thought. We used to go to a Congregational church—no, wait a minute, I think it may have been Presbyterian—but that was a long time ago. How about you, Angie?" he asked naughtily, the only one who could get away with using the nickname Angela loathed, as it made her feel "rather like a Sicilian bimbo."

"Let's say I'm comfortably ecumenical, dear. A certain 'when in Rome' outlook on the divine, I suppose. I rather fancy I could become a bit of a Buddhist, though, if I were very long in Bangkok or Burma, or wherever it is the Buddhists hang their little square hats. Such charming accoutrements to the faith, don't you think? This lovely thing, for instance," she said, lifting her jade pendant. "My ex-husband got it for me when we were somewhere in Southeast Asia. He persuaded a terribly sweet little Buddhist monk to appropriate it from the local temple in exchange for a small contribution to the faithful. Charming man. And I so love jade."

"*It's all those fuckin' Rockefellers' fault!*" interrupted a very drunk man with an Irish brogue who had nearly fallen over their table. "It's on account of them that this fuckin' Kissinger started this fuckin' war with the fuckin' A-rabs. *That's* why you're gonna be payin' more for your fuckin' oil. *That's* why," he said, tapping a front-page newspaper picture of the secretary of state and the governor of New York and thrusting it under Angela's nose.

Artie was alarmed. Elizabeth rolled her eyes. Richard, thinking his recently exercised body might be called into protective action—particularly if the drunk got an earful of Angela's British accent—roused himself to an unusual state of alertness.

"Really, love," said Angela, more emphatically English than ever, pretending great interest in the Irishman's analysis. "Do let me have a further look," she said, taking the paper from him. The Irishman waited mutely as she opened it up. It was not, however, to the editorial page that she turned. It was to the entertainment section. "Oh, look," she said, pointing the Irishman's attention to the listings. "What a lovely film is playing just across the street at the Orson Welles. Now why don't you take yourself there and have a wonderful time, and come back here about, oh, say one o'clock? That will give the four of us enough time in which to discuss your fascinating appraisal of the international situation so that we can then go over it with you on your level. Until then, I'm afraid you'd be terribly bored with us. You *will* allow us this time to prepare, won't you? Oh, good. I knew you would," she said, folding up the paper and handing it back to him. "Do enjoy the film. We'll be so eager to talk to you later."

The Irishman looked at Angela in reverent confusion, then turned and stumbled away.

"There," said Angela, as soon as he was a safe distance from their table. "Actually, perhaps it wouldn't be such a bad idea for us all to push off," she said, smiling broadly at Artie, whose stomach flipped with the implication of her suggestion. "This place is getting impossibly crowded," she explained, "so why don't we settle up?" As they all went to their wallets and pockets, Angela leaned over to Artie and whispered, "And since there's no more room here at the inn, love, what do you say to our repairing to the manger?"

Artie dropped two quarters on the floor and then managed to nod.

Richard was going back to Elizabeth's for coffee. When Angela let the two of them out of her BMW on Putnam Avenue, she lilted, "See you soon, shock troops! Be getting in shape for the Houghton!" This envoi troubled Artie, indicating as it did the possibility of something awful happening in the building of his worst fears. But he was so preoccupied with what was about to happen tonight that there seemed no point in questioning whatever she might have in store for him next week.

"Well," he said, feigning lightheartedness after Elizabeth and Richard had left, "your place or mine?"

"Goodness, darling, do you have to ask? I wouldn't be caught dead in yours, although I was rather taken with the enormous man to whom I handed your Greek book on Monday."

"He's gay," Artie informed her.

"Is he?" Angela asked. "He must be the only one who is in this gruesome town."

When Angela snapped on the light in her living room, Artie's eye accidentally traveled to her bound master's thesis, "Conventions of Rejection," and he wondered if this was perhaps a bad omen for things they were only about to begin.

"Nervous, darling?" she inquired, going off into the kitchen to make drinks.

"Oh, no, I'm not nervous," Artie answered, his eyes darting around the room. "Oh, Angela, don't fix anything for me. I really don't need anything more."

" 'Provokes the desire, but it takes away the performance,' is that it, love?"

"Certainly not," Artie protested, unwilling to be unmanned by even so formidable a combination as Angela and *Macbeth*.

"Well, I myself prefer to keep the engine running with a bit of a refill," she countered.

Artie, still a little insulted, responded, "Suit yourself."

Actually, what she now began to do was unsuit him. Maneuvering him to the sofa after a few swigs of vodka-and-vodka, Angela quickly unbuttoned and removed his shirt and began systematically kissing him: first on the mouth, then on the neck, then on his nipples, then in several places on his quite hairless chest, followed by a detour to his ribs and ending with some last smooches on his flat belly.

"Now, darling, isn't this rather more therapeutic than what you do with Mrs. . . . Cringle?" she asked.

Artie didn't say a word. Nor did he move a muscle except for those responding involuntarily in the pelvic region.

"Really, darling," whispered Angela, who was now working expertly on his left ear, "you might say or do *some*thing. I do think it would make me feel a bit less likely to be arrested for child molestation in the morning. Aren't you enjoying yourself?"

Artie's tongue was locked not by second thoughts but by desire. His body was filled with sensations that had never before been approximated in him. He thought he might swoon.

Instead, however, he burst forth in a Pentecostal flood of Keats: " 'O Attic shape! Fair attitude!' Yes! Enjoying myself? I'm so excited I can hardly talk! If I'm silent, it's only from 'being too happy in thine happiness.' " His mouth made a sharp right turn for Angela's, depriving her of his ear. His hands began grasping and releasing furiously—breasts, face, arms, waist. Attempting to push Angela down on her back, he knocked a porcelain ashtray off her coffee table and onto the Oriental rug.

"Darling," she pointed out. "The bed is forty-nine feet square, whereas the couch is perhaps a mere fifteen. Shall we go into the bedroom?"

Artie, his mouth once again frozen with ardor, nodded vigorously. So eager was he to get to the bedroom that he ran into it ahead of Angela, as if she were someone he had passed chasing a bus.

Now thoroughly enjoying herself, Angela followed, quoting Donne and unbuttoning her blouse:

> *"These burning fits but meteors be,*
> *Whose matter in thee is soon spent."*

Somewhat to her surprise, Artie was able to respond with the next lines, and they turned "A Fever" into a dialogue:

> *"Thy beauty and all parts which are thee*
> *Are unchangeable firmament,"*

he said, fervently.

> *"Yet 'twas of my mind, seizing thee,*
> *Though it in thee cannot persever,"*

she continued.

This sounded inauspicious, but deciding this was no time for exegesis, and for once in his life determined to be the grasshopper and not the ant, he concluded:

> *"For I had rather owner be*
> *Of thee one houre, than all else ever."*

As this final rhyme sounded, they were both at last lying on Angela's bed. "Lovely," she said, complimenting his recitation. "But don't you think this will all work much better if you remove those sweet little blue jeans?"

9

Artie spent most of the weekend reading Henry James and trying to catch up on the Greek he had let slide since Angela became the textbook's alpha and omega. Early darkness over the North Yard assisted his efforts at buckling down, though the loud sounds of the law school mixer on Saturday night—he had spied Freddie guiding his very blond, very Pine-Manor-Junior-College date up Oxford Street—were a distraction. Also getting in the way of studiousness was his newfound lust. Far from exhausting his physical desires, his Friday night with Angela had left him eager for more. He even wondered if his natural ardor might be exceptional: he rather liked the idea of himself as a wild man. But Angela had said no to any further contact between them until Sunday night—"I have some perfectly exhausting shopping to do Saturday, and besides, I don't want you getting behind in your reading of the literature of the frontier." So Artie waited and read, finding the heroes of Henry James more bloodless, and their problems more pointless, than he would have just two days before.

On his way out Sunday night, he noticed that a regulation dormitory chair had been set out in the corridor by the Gainsborough boy's room for Juan to dispose of in the morning. Its vinyl seat was split. Gobs of beige stuffing foamed from the crack. Artie surmised that the couplings of the Pithecanthropus and his partner had now succeeded in breaking furniture. To this rugged sight, as to the fiction of Henry James, Artie's response was not what it would have been forty-eight hours before. Then he would have been startled, even appalled; but now, on his way to Angela's, he looked upon the battered chair with fond acceptance. It was a casualty of love, a little hamlet the troops of Eros had made a mess of while marching down the highway to fulfillment. It was like Angela's ashtray, which on Friday night would have smashed to pieces had it not been for the thickness of her Oriental carpet. Artie looked at that chair now and he *knew*. A Ph.D. candidate in anthropology who lived on the first floor was making a study of kinship systems based on behavioral affinities rather than genes. He might have taken note of this new rapport between Artie, the Gainsborough boy and the Pithecanthropus. Artie himself now realized how those who are getting it are profoundly separate from those who are not; how the gulf between the erotically enfranchised and sexually deprived is perhaps wider than any resulting from race, creed or national origin. Being more secret, he reflected, it is also more bitter. All the world does not love a lover; in fact, only other lovers do.

In novels, new male lovers often have a "spring in their step." Artie's stride underwent a more significant change. It was now executed, as he made his way to Angela's, with only one hand in his pocket. The other swung by his side with what might almost be called abandon. He was still going through plenty of "supposes" and over-the-shoulder checks—his collar size was increasing with new muscular development—but the change was encouraging.

"I ought to charge you by the pound," the barber growled, hewing down another tuft of Artie's hair. He wasn't used to extreme cases like this one coming into the business school shop. Clipping to the converted, the twice-monthly trim, was really his line. He figured it could only be the blonde sitting in the chair with a magazine who had got this guy to take his mop across the river and give it up.

Artie winced. He was thinking about his hair, which he would miss. He was thinking about the annoyed barber. He was thinking about Samson and Delilah. It was Saturday, just eight days after they'd first made love, and Angela was getting him to do this. He looked in the mirror and saw her, still intent on this month's *Forbes* and refusing to look up until it was over—until he had a part, a back to his neck, ears. It was the first step in a makeover to which he had assented on the condition that Angela let him pay her back out of his next fellowship check, not due for months.

She had insisted on a haircut first—"a minimal prerequisite to clothes shopping, darling, like clean underwear before an accident." From the B-school barber they proceeded to Crimson Shoes, Ltd., "Booters to Gentlemen." Artie's high-top Keds gave way to brown leather oxfords. "A little less point to the toe, I think," Angela told the salesman, rejecting one pair for another that had a millimeter or two more width in front. The salesman ignored Artie totally, making him feel like a Korean orphan who'd been brought to the States for surgery.

"Now, love," Angela said when they were back out in the Square, "on to Boston. For the entrée." They walked toward the kiosk, and Artie made for the steps leading down to the subway. "Don't make bad jokes," Angela said, tugging on what was left of his hair. She steered him to the row of cabs.

A couple of blocks from Brooks Brothers on Newbury Street, as they waited for a light, Angela came close to shouting. "*There*," she said, "right *there*," pointing to someone crossing the street.

"Who's that?" Artie asked.

"You," she answered. "About an hour from now." The man was about Artie's height, same coloring, just a little heavier and older. He had a business suit on underneath a sporty trench coat. Angela appeared deeply interested in him. Artie wondered why anyone would need to dress that way on a Saturday morning.

They took an elevator to the suits floor. On the way up Artie pondered the Brooks Brothers logo, that little sheep in a sling.

He wondered if that's where he was being put, already shorn. Out on the selling floor he was startled by the sheer number of groomed, deodorized and discerning young males, all shopping for what seemed to be the same gray pair of pants.

"This is amazing," he whispered to Angela.

"However so?" she asked.

"I mean all these guys who look like this. It's as if the last ten years had never happened."

"If only they hadn't," Angela said. "Fortunately, they're over. This is the future, darling. Believe me. The past has only been playing possum. Soon there will be no more tambourine men. You might as well greet the brave old world in style."

This gave Artie a certain you're-in-the-army-now sensation, and, taking off his jeans in one of the dressing rooms, he felt as if he were waiting to see a doctor instead of a salesman. But he had to admit there was something he liked about the place: the quiet, the smell, Angela's evident approval. Without her here he would have felt like a scholarship boy, an interloper; with her he seemed to have unlimited credit, social as well as financial.

"What do you think?" he said, emerging from the cubicle with dark blue gabardine drooping over his wrists and ankles. Angela saw through the ridiculousness to the finished product. "It will be perfect," she pronounced. She turned to the salesman and said, delightedly, "Yes. Please take us to the man who'll put the little chalk marks all over him."

While the fitter turned Artie this way and that in front of the mirrors, Angela held two ties against his shirt front. One was blue with little white dots; the other, red with little white dots. She kept alternating them, unable to make up her mind. Artie was surprised to find himself joining in the intent comparison. Even though he still needed to have as much gabardine hacked away from him as he had had hair, he was amazed at how good he looked, how right the whole effect would be.

"Maybe we could get both of them?" he asked, a little timidly.

Angela broke into a huge smile. "Oh, darling, that's the most wonderful thing I've ever heard you say!"

"I don't know. I mean, this has only been going on for about ten days, but I feel like my life has been changed. It's overwhelming. But I don't know if it's right. It was so unexpected. I mean, I don't even know if I'm in love with her. All I know is she overpowers me. I don't think she's in love with me. I mean, how could she be? She's so amazing, and I'm so, you know, nothing. I don't know if I should be doing this. It seems so crazy, but also so . . ."

"Wonderful, maybe?" Mrs. Crangel asked.

"Yes," said Artie. "But scary, too."

"Are you eating these days?"

"Yes, much better, thank you."

"Looking over your shoulder a little less? Thinking less frequently about all the catastrophes that could be involved in walking from A to B?"

"Yes. Maybe about half as much for both of those things."

"Sounds like a miracle to me," Mrs. Crangel smiled.

He wished she wouldn't laugh at him.

"Well, I *am* still thinking a lot of that crazy stuff."

"But less, no?"

"Yes, less."

"Don't tell me you've gone from complete despair to having unreasonable expectations in just a week!"

"No," said Artie. "I'm sorry. I realize I should be grateful."

"Why be grateful? Why not just be glad?"

This sounded vaguely immoral, irreligious, to Artie. He didn't answer.

"Why do you have to decide right away whether or not you're in love with Angela?" Mrs. Crangel persisted. "Is there anything wrong with just being happy and busy for a while?"

"No," Artie conceded. "But what about the big questions we

talked about last week? Isn't whether or not I'm in love one of them? If I keep making mindless love to Angela, won't I still be avoiding them? Won't it be just like thinking about the demons instead of getting the big answers?"

"Arthur," Mrs. Crangel responded, "there is a great deal of difference between putting your hands on Angela and putting your hands in your pockets. One is real; the other isn't."

Artie blushed. Mrs. Crangel pressed on: "I'm not telling you to duck the big questions. But why not gather a little more data before trying to answer them? Be more inductive. Reason your way from the particulars to the general. Angela sounds like a very attractive set of particulars to be working with at the moment."

Artie paused and then answered. "I know you're right. But I'm so confused. I worry all day about work, and the future, and crossing the street, and then I show up at her apartment and I forget about everything except doing it. Sorry," he added, afraid he had put it too crassly.

"Arthur, I'm afraid your problem at the moment is that you're experiencing the very last thing your nature wants to let you experience."

"What's that?"

"A good time."

The special session of the Symposium, the one dealing with Dryden's literary remains, met at 3:00 on Friday in a corner of the Houghton's reading room. Artie's stomach felt queasy, because he knew Angela had her "little surprise" planned for this afternoon. And despite all his pleading in bed the night before, she had refused to reveal what it was. "But Richard and Elizabeth know," he had protested. "Ah, love, this is your penalty for rushing off to make an appointment with Mrs. Cringle that evening *we* all went to the Blue Parrot," she reminded him. "Just wait. You'll see, sweetie."

Canker had had the members of the Symposium gather around

two tables on which had been laid out various bits of Drydeniana. He stood at the far end of one of them; Branded was seated at his right. From where Artie was sitting, the great golden minute hand of the reading room's clock seemed to be making its way, like Damocles' sword, for the right side of Canker's head. By 3:40, Artie figured out, he would be able to pretend its sweep had completely decapitated him. By concentrating on this game, he hoped to keep his mind off Angela's impending guerrilla action, whatever it might be. It was odd, though, how wondering about her apparently real plans was actually less scary than all his recent imaginings of pillage and plunder in this room. "*One is real, the other isn't.*"

Canker was marveling about "the man whose ephemerae we have before us, the man who gave us the great 'Mac Flecknoe,' 'Religio Laici' and 'Essay of Dramatic Poesy,' whose refusal to swear oaths during the revolution lost him the poet laureateship." Little Nell regarded the detritus of Dryden's busy life with moist, sympathetic eyes. Branded looked not at the items on the table but at Canker. The eyes of the others wandered the walls from portrait to portrait. Elizabeth yawned. Richard did a flexing exercise with his wrists. Angela gaily waved to the library's director as he passed through the reading room with one of his daughter-in-law's cookies in his mouth. Artie's eyes went back and forth from the clock to Angela.

At 3:55, long after Canker had been done in by the sweep of the clock's minute hand, there was a long, awful shriek from the other end of the reading room. Words began to emerge from the screams: "I hate him! I *hate* him! I HATE *T. S. ELIOT!*" shouted a young man who appeared to be an undergraduate and who must have been given access to the Houghton's manuscripts by some privileged arrangement. "I HATE HIM!" he cried one last time before picking up a pile of papers from the table and ripping them, first in half, then into quarters, then into confetti.

The desk attendants froze. Canker exhaled as if he'd been

punched in the stomach. Branded didn't know what to worry about first, the shredded manuscripts or his mentor's respiration. Little Nell, in horror, brought her hands to her face, smearing her blush-on.

Finally, a male attendant came flying around the desk toward the student, and Branded dove for the table with the torn papers like a paratrooper hitting the beach. But before either could get to him, the student escaped.

Branded surveyed the wreckage as everyone waited to hear which gloomy classics of twentieth-century poetry had just perished. After turning over several of the ripped bits, he announced disbelievingly, "It's only blank paper. It's only typing paper from the Coop!" Everyone sighed. Canker ran up to Branded and flung his arms around him. Too moved to speak, he dismissed the class with a joyful wave. Little Nell reached her stained hands heavenward.

Once outside the building, Artie looked dumbfoundedly at Angela.

"Oh, love, it was easy," she responded. "I just proposed it to this swift-footed undergraduate I found, and he was quite willing to do it. I gave him a rather generous fee."

"But what if he gets expelled?"

"Oh, nonsense. For what? For ripping up a fifty-nine-cent tablet? For having an attack of the screamies? They'll just have his proctor send him to bed with a glass of warm milk—if they ever even find him."

"But they *will* find him," Artie worried. "He had to register with the reading room, didn't he?"

"Yes, he did. Under the name of F. R. Leavis. I suppose the attendant must simply not have checked it against his bursar's card," Angela said.

Artie persisted: "But one of the attendants still had to push the button at the desk to unlock the door for him to get out!"

"As a matter of fact, you're right, darling. She did. It was that lovely old callipygian frau. I mentioned all this to her the other day. She decided it would be a bit of fun."

The next morning they rose early.

"Relax, Angela. There's no need to get pissed. We're nearly at the pump. Everybody's in the same boat."

"Wrong," she said, pointlessly gunning the engine as she kept her other foot on the brake. "I am not pissed. 'Pissed' means intoxicated. The expression you're seeking is 'cheesed off.' And furthermore, none of us is in a boat. What we're all in is this bloody queue."

Artie was determined to keep his good mood. The world might be browned out and cheesed off from Pittsburgh to Piccadilly, but he had blessings to count. Despite everything, even stunts like yesterday's, he was less nervous than a month ago. He had Angela. He had Mrs. Crangel. He had Elizabeth and Richard.

He honked Angela's horn, smiling.

"Now what good will that do?" she asked.

"You're supposed to," he said. "See?" He pointed to the bumper sticker on the car in front of them: HONK IF YOU'RE FOR IMPEACHMENT.

Angela gave him a look of severe disgust. "Keep your seditious thoughts to yourself. And keep your mangy little paws off my hooter."

Her feelings toward sedition were selective. Resigned to another few minutes of immobility, she went back to reading Antonia Fraser's new biography of Cromwell. "Where is he when we need him?" she asked, pointing to the newsmagazine in Artie's lap. Princess Anne was getting married that month, and there were color pictures of her and Captain Phillips. "Have you ever seen such a look of equine equanimity?"

The attendant at last waved them to the pump. The numbers flew by on the meter, and Artie pondered the soon-to-be Phillipses. He and Mark were both lucky guys, he decided. But he was even luckier. Angela was miles ahead of Princess Anne in looks—brains, too. How had he done it? The question made him insecure, so he concentrated on just feeling lucky. Mrs. Crangel would want it that way.

Angela zoomed out of the station, but after going half a block, she put her car on another line, shorter this time, that had formed near a vacant lot. A teenager was selling two-gallon drums of gasoline for people to put in their trunks.

"It's illegal," Artie said. "You could blow up."

"Darling, it's your turn to relax."

Artie decided to agree. He went back to thinking lucky, not insecure. He lowered himself in the seat and stretched. Looking right, he saw a woman in the next car reading *I'm O.K., You're O.K.* between inchings toward the contraband.

I'm O.K., You're O.K. Artie closed his eyes and recited the phrase to himself like a mantra. He breathed deeply. It was a crisp November morning. *I'm O.K., You're O.K.* He had chocolate chip cookies in his book bag. *I'm O.K., You're O.K.* He and Angela had made love an hour ago. *I'm O.K., You're O.K.* He smiled. His eyes still closed, he mumbled dreamily, "Angela?"

"Yes, love?"

"I'm okay. You're okay."

"Don't bet on it," she replied.

Bogus Hall
November 18, 1973

Dear Shane,

Just as you predicted, I was on the A list. I mean Angela and I are having an affair. Do people still use that term? I know what participle you would use, but somehow I can't. And yet I wonder if that's maybe all we're doing, impure and simple. I mean I don't know if I love her—and I don't think she's in love with me—both of us never really use that expression—but I don't know how to resist her. I don't know if I'm doing the right thing or not. I wish you were here to give me some advice.

She does these things I just can't do back. When she wants to go to bed, she'll just suddenly look at me and say "Anyone for tennis?" She did this the other day in the lunch room in Lehman Hall at a very high volume. It was a gray, slushy, wet day, so I mean everybody knew she couldn't really be talking about tennis. (Although I guess some people really do play tennis indoors, don't they?) She just kind of expected me to get up and walk out with her. And I did. And then we did. Did "it," I mean.

The other day I thought she was going to set fire to the rare book library here. Actually, she just set in motion a kind of practical joke to scare Canker and his creepy disciple. In some ways it was pretty funny, and they really did get scared, but I don't know. When we were rehashing it at her apartment that night, she was already bored with it while I was still having a nervous breakdown, and I hadn't even done anything. Richard —a friend of ours here—says, "She's great. She's like a cross between Catherine the Great and Winnie Ruth Judd." Well, I know about Catherine (even the horse), but I'd never heard of Winnie, so I asked him. She was the "trunk murderess."

Shane, I wish I could see you. I'm less nuts (sorry, fucked-up) than I was a month ago—in fact, there are moments when she makes me amazingly happy—but so many things are still driving me crazy. (Is *that* word okay?) What am I doing trying to read Greek, Henry Vaughan, Henry James and Shelley's "Defence of Poesy" and construct a bibliographical description of a phony quarto of *The Merry Wives of Windsor* in one day for? I really did all these things today, but they just add up to a great cloud of unknowing. This is literature? Maybe Freddie is better off after all. At least he knows what he wants. I ran into him today. He's already looking for summer jobs with law firms in New York. He had on a button that said, "Free the Fortune 500!"

I don't know if over here in the graduate school we're more "sensitive" to the higher things in life than the law school guys are, or just so out of it we wouldn't know the high from the low.

Tonight in the lounge, when we were all getting set to watch the news, an argument broke out about whether we should tune to NBC or CBS. After a few minutes of this, Voltears, who usually sails through the hall on a sniffling puddle, suddenly jumped up and screamed, "You'll watch CBS and you'll like it, you motherfuckers!"

In any case, I'm off to Angela's later, which is better than sleeping here. June 28th is 225 days away, and I hope they go fast. Please write or call again. If not for me, then for the Blue Boy, who usually answers the phone—

I miss you—

Artie

Each time one of Artie's oxfords landed on the dance floor it would stick, or twist in the wrong direction, and be unable to connect its movement in any purposeful way to the previous step or the one to come. But he was trying. His newly short hair was shaking and his thin arms were flailing. Alas, he was missing the point: in the nascent post-rock realm of disco one was supposed to undulate, not shake; slither, not flail.

Angela, who had driven him, Richard and Elizabeth into Boston to a new place called Satan, had picked up the proper technique immediately. Even so, she seemed to be deriving more pleasure from Artie's appearance than her own prowess. Yet another shirt she had bought him ("Too late, love; I know the size now") was tucked into the "sweet little blue jeans" she still let him wear, and at which Satan's Friday-night Cerberus had scowled. As Artie moved ineptly under the pink strobe lights, Angela boogied automatically and laughed. "Really, darling," she shouted into the clamor, "you look as if you're suffering from one of those diseases for which they give those telethons on the box." Artie, who failed to hear her, smiled and nodded thanks. He was a little drunk and feeling proud to be with her and eager to release the frustrations of another week at Harvard. Despite his lingering fears, he was determined to get, more or less, down.

He inched closer to her and, pointing to Elizabeth and Richard at their table, yelled, "Do you think they're what you'd call an item? Like us?" he asked.

"Is that what we are?" Angela questioned loudly.

"Sure. Aren't we?" Artie shouted.

"Darling, you make us sound like a tin of baking soda. As for Elizabeth and Richard—no, I should think not."

"Why not?" Artie screamed, as the record said *like you baby like you baby* for the sixty-second time.

"Because Richard's libido is insufficiently energetic for Elizabeth, who is secretly a virago, just like myself."

Artie considered this, wondering how Angela could manage to remain both polysyllabic and grammatical in this boiler room. "He's not like my little Tigger," she said, moving closer to Artie as she used her *Pooh* name for him and squeezing the inside of his right thigh.

Artie flinched. Why *did* she insist on doing things like that? he wondered, looking around him, worried that someone had seen her, unaware that within thirty feet of them were occurring two illegal drug transactions and one act of fellatio. He stepped back to resume his chaste shaking and flailing.

Angela's forty-nine-square-foot bed was strewn with biographies of Elizabethan poets, Ian Fleming novels, her body and Artie's. She was half asleep. He was wide awake and wondering: why did she want him? They seemed about as equal as her BMW and his Schwinn. Did she want to mother him? Torture him? Perhaps love him? For days he had wanted to utter those explosive words, "Let's talk about us," but he sensed that if he did, she would fix him with her laser look. He settled for asking, "What are you thinking about?"

Angela roused slightly and turned her head toward him, her blond hair swirling marvelously on the pillow.

"Oh, is that you, love? Actually, my state of wakefulness was such that I'm not quite sure whether I was thinking or merely dreaming, but the last picture in my mind was of the ducks under Magdalene Bridge."

"You mean in Cambridge?" Artie asked.

"That's right, love. The other one. The real one."

"Why were you thinking of them? Or dreaming about them."

"Well, love, I don't know," she answered, her whisper betraying a surprisingly real interest in the question he had asked. "I suppose I miss them. I used to pass them several times a week, and whenever I did I'd wave to them rather cheerfully. I suppose," she added, a new note of wistfulness entering her voice, "that I miss the whole place. Being able to disappear for days and weeks at a time, telling one's supervisor one had missed an appointment because one had been called away to Pago Pago or someplace like that. Over here this absurd business of 'classes' makes one feel back in the sixth form. I suppose I miss the freedom of it all." She paused and then continued. "I also miss things like King's College Chapel cutting into the night sky, the little vessels on the roof of the Senate House being swept over by the clouds."

This was the closest Artie had ever heard her come to making a sentimental remark. He found it distantly threatening. Then, as if she too knew she was in alien territory, Angela pulled back. Changing moods, and putting her arms around Artie's chest, she asked, in her usual Angela voice, "Now, love, do you suppose that when we do it this time, you might hold onto my shoulders a bit less as if you're clinging to the last pontoon out of Dunkirk?"

"That's the kind of remark," said an awed Joseph Branded, "that can make one think about literature—or even life—in a wholly new way."

The Symposium was discussing Matthew Arnold this afternoon, so the connection of literature and life was inevitable. The only problem with Branded's appreciation was that the remark he was alluding to was not one of Arnold's but merely one of Canker's own observations on the text at hand, a typical blank charge fired off the cuff. Now that it was well into November, no one but Branded and Canker, and sometimes Little Nell, made more than the weakest pretense of being interested in what transpired afternoons in Warble House. Angela buffed her nails; Richard played tic-tac-toe with himself.

Artie wasn't engaged, but he was still unable to break his lifetime habits of conscientiousness, and try as he might to tune out, some bits of Arnold's verse and prose, transmitted through the mouth of Canker, reached his ears and registered:

> *Business could not make dull, nor passion wild;*
> *Who saw life steadily, and saw it whole . . .*

If you thought about it, Artie mused, Sophocles, Arnold's subject here, was a lot like Mrs. Crangel. She saw life steadily and whole. But she wasn't opposed to your seeing it in parts if that was all you could manage at the moment. Eventually, she tried to make you feel, things would add up. Artie wondered if he was really going to get it all straightened out.

> *. . . this strange disease of modern life,*
> *With its sick hurry, its divided aims . . .*

You're not kidding, divided. This weekend meant sentences from Herodotus, poems by Southwell, a novel by William Dean Howells, essays by Ruskin, and researching the use of cow urine in the marbled designs on the endpapers of Victorian books. And between threads of this lunatic weave he was supposed to have dinner with Freddie and go on another shopping expedition with Angela, who insisted that both she and the economy needed stimulation.

" . . . poetry is at bottom a criticism of life. . ." There: the key sentence had at last come into what might charitably be called the class's discussion. Literature and life, Artie thought. He did believe in their marriage—ardently, in fact. They belonged together, like Romulus and Remus, Thames and Medway, Frank and Joe Hardy. He loved books and poems that were of and about the world, that helped you to live in it, told you how. The 1970s were said to be the great age of the self-help book, but to Artie's mind all books were self-help books, or at least ought to be. He hated clever postmodern Pynchonian puzzle-novels, Nabokovian books about writing books, "concrete poetry" without theme or meaning. In all this he was, in fact, at one with the party line as it came down through Canker, who fancied himself a gallant humanist doing battle with the brute and sterile cruelties of life in the late-twentieth century. The only trouble was that Canker wouldn't know life if it smacked him between the shoulder blades. He thought Harvard was life, and that all beyond its gates was quicksand—uneducated, undifferentiated, without hope. Books, as a consequence, became things for the lucky to hoard and categorize, but never really to use.

If, Artie hypothesized, he was suddenly to raise his hand and actually start relating literature to life as it was being lived by the members of the Symposium, Canker and Branded would be aghast. "Okay, everybody!" he imagined himself shouting in an academic coup d'état. "Literature and life! Here they come! Richard! Suppose you tell us about the 'Ode to Indolence'—you must know more about that than anyone. Angela! Tell us why half the stuff Enobarbus said Cleopatra had on her barge is strictly Woolworth's compared to what's in your apartment. Hey! I just read some of Donne's 'Holy Sonnets.' What do you all think? Does God exist or not?" Even with Herman Howell, could one imagine talking about the bedrock matter of the poems at hand? Could one move the discussion from form and doctrine to the question of whether or not the people sitting there reading the poem believed in God themselves? Nothing would be more guaranteed to stop conversation.

It wasn't Little Nell's rhapsodies about poems and poets Artie wanted; it was something hot and exciting—namely, to stir literature into the cauldron of life, to make it not only please but nourish, to see if it couldn't help them all *to come up with some answers*. And yet to make such a point in this room—despite all the official homage being paid Arnold—would be to declare himself a weirdo. But why? Artie thought. They had all the answers right in their laps, resting between all the covers of all these anthologies. Surely, even Mrs. Crangel couldn't know as much. Why did they so perversely refuse to use what was here? How could it be that handsome Jeffrey Stanhope taught these books all morning and then still had to go to the psychiatrist in the afternoon? Had they all lost their nerve? Had they all given up? Angela was still at her nails; Richard was surreptitiously blowing Bazooka bubble gum bubbles; even Artie himself, for all his agitation, was just doodling swirls in his notebook.

Only Elizabeth, he noticed, had a truly composed and alert expression on her face. And then he saw why. She was reading. She had a copy of *I Promessi Sposi* inconspicuously on her lap. Her eyes were avidly moving from line to line. Artie wondered if she would ever apply this particular book to her own life. He doubted it—she didn't strike him as the marrying kind. He wondered, in fact, why she was reading it at all—she wasn't taking an Italian course. And then he realized why she had the book in her lap. She had it for a reason they had all misplaced months ago, when they came here, a reason she must somehow, temporarily, have relocated.

She was reading the book because she wanted to.

Urnino,

What Mild Bill actually does is sell computer crap to semi-big businessmen. Which means I spend large portions of my day pushing these buttons I don't know fuck-all about and making little green numbers come up on a screen. Then I tell these weenies who make Rustoleum or land-based missiles or whatever the fuck they happen to make just how much "hardware" they need, and just how much "software" they need to go with it.

Between weenies I blow joints in the can. Then I get home

and eat at Mild Bill's, which is less pleasure than necessity, he having given me about ⅓ of a paycheck so far. After that I go out to find Erin, who was the girlfriend I had the last time I was out here and whom I was interested in recycling this trip. Love, I've decided, it's not, but she still manages to turn my software to hardware (yuk, yuk—*laugh*, you goddamned little bookmonger).

As for your own chick, this Downing job. I don't know, Urn Man. She sounds like a potential dragon lady. I'd advise you to keep your little ceramic ass covered. I always figured you for quiet types like Katharine. Ah, what the fuck, enjoy being an *homme fatal*.

Maybe it's my turn for a nervous breakdown. The fuck out of here is where I want to get. Meanwhile, I'm off to Erin's with a bottle of rosé and some mesc.

Stay the fuck out of trouble—
Shane

P.S. Tell Blue Boy I'm not easy.

10

Two nights before Thanksgiving Artie was in the Comus TV room with the Chinese physics student. Artie had arrived second, so the choice of program was already made: a rerun episode of *An American Family*, starring the real-life Louds of Santa Barbara, California.

Talk about literature and life. If you could call video a form of literature, then here the barrier between it and life practically disappeared. How, Artie and the nation had wondered, could these people have allowed the camera to follow them around from room to room, day after day, catching every itch and scratch? The Louds were often discussed on late-night radio call-in shows, which Artie listened to on certain sleepless nights when he was here instead of at Angela's. One person from the North End would call the host and say that the family's troubles were all brought on by "that fruity kid," and then somebody from Brighton would rebut this and say that if the family weren't so screwed up, the kid wouldn't be so fruity. "And the mother ought to cut her *hair*," a woman hissed one morning at 2 A.M. "Past forty. Who does she think she is?"

Margaret Mead had pronounced the series' technique "the most important event in human thought since the invention of the novel." Artie had mentioned this to Angela one night in bed; he knew it would provoke her, though not exactly in the way it did. "Oh, the novel," she said wearily, making him recall how she found it a genre that hadn't quite proved itself, even in its third century of test marketing.

It was by her tastes, Artie realized, that he chiefly knew Angela. Seventeenth-century English poetry was good. Hour-long American TV series about forensic medicine were good. Harvard was bad. So were sequined tee shirts (fashionable that fall) and the British Labour Party. Having her right ear licked ("darling, you're *much* better at that than you were just a week ago") was good. What if, he feared, that was really all there was to her—a collection of arbitrary tastes, all promulgated with stylish absolutism? The tastes might be like spring water, all bubbly and bracing, but was there some bedrock of values beneath?

He still knew almost nothing of her history. A few attempts to get her to talk about her past, beyond what she'd said the afternoon they divided up the syllabus in her apartment, had been futile. "Life begins with divorce," she said, and as far as Artie knew, that was still the real beginning of her *vita*. He had speculated, of course, though only to himself, afraid she might get wind of any hypothesizing he did with, say, Elizabeth. He wondered now if he wouldn't someday discover that she'd been born into a family of mill workers in Manchester, with howling working-class vowels and a daddy who beat up on mum before going off to darts at the pub. Maybe she really owed her current regal airs and bank book to the kind of transformation one finds in the novels she professed to dislike. Someone had discovered a strawberry mark on her ankle, proving her a duke's daughter (eighteenth-century plot twist). Or she had started a little pork-pie stand near the factory gate, and it had grown into a million-pound-a-year business (nineteenth-century paradigm). But he knew her ankles were alabaster and that she couldn't light a stove.

He stopped pondering when Mr. and Mrs. Loud increased their poolside abuse of each other to unusual volume. He winced for them and decided to go back upstairs. Besides, whatever Margaret Mead might think, there were higher priorities: he had to go read about the Snopeses and Compsons for Angela's summary. Getting up from the couch, he smiled at the Chinese physics student, who looked puzzled. "Leaving?" he said.

"Got to," Artie replied.

"I always stay to the end," the other explained. "Like to watch them. Nice family. Make me less homesick."

"I really cannot see the point of annually ingesting these absurd quantities of forest food," Angela grumbled as her fork sliced through a sweet potato. She was in a bad humor because most of the regular television schedule had been canceled for Thanksgiving football games. "Why aren't you all home, in any case?" she asked Artie, Richard and Elizabeth. "We don't *have* this silly gourmandising holiday where I come from. But why haven't you gathered around your families' no doubt buckling dining room tables instead of insisting I come with you to this dark little restaurant? It's very discouraging. Everyone here seems horribly lonely," she said, making a panning gesture with her yam-stained fork.

"Well, we're lonely, too," Artie responded, a little surprised at his own words. Maybe he looked in every so often on the Louds for the same reason the Chinese physics student did.

"Oh, stuff," Angela said. "If you're so lonely, why aren't you home?"

"Because," Artie explained, "if I went home for Thanksgiving, my mom and dad would expect me to stay for the whole weekend, and I couldn't. I've got Southwell, Thoreau, T. S. Eliot and Greek to read. Once I got down there I'd never be able to break away. I don't even know how I'm finding the time to do this," he complained, going to work on his cranberries with accelerated speed.

"Or to do anything else," Angela added. Last night she had, after reading some of Sidney's *Arcadia* and watching *Marcus Welby, M.D.*, waited for him to come over, as they had planned.

He had called her at eleven from Comus, in a panic over undone work, to cancel. She had been less than perfectly understanding.

"Richard?" she asked. Whenever Angela started one of her round-robin questions, she expected everyone to follow through with an answer.

"I'm not sure my parents are home," he replied. "I think my father's in Indonesia on some congressional thing. My mother is with him, I think, but she could be in New Mexico with her boyfriend. If I'd gone home, I probably would've found the house empty."

"Understandable," Angela averred. She looked to Elizabeth.

"A few weeks from now is Chanukah. If you think I'm facing all that *Gemeinschaft Schmalz* twice in one month, you're out of your tree, Downing."

Angela nodded. She grudgingly let them go back to the food they were eating much more heartily than she was. Elizabeth and Artie, who were splurging far beyond their budgets, went at their meals with particular intensity. When they finished, Angela waited impatiently for the waitress to clear the plates.

"Now for pumpkin pie," said Elizabeth.

"Oh, Lord," said Angela. "When does all this end?"

"With the mints, Angie," said Richard.

"Brought to us in a wicker basket by Squanto the pilgrim, no doubt. Really, I am amazed at the ability of this disgusting national spree to turn even the most emaciated of you into gluttons." They all looked at Artie, who was doing so well with his food that he wished Shane or his mother were there to observe.

"I'll wait until you've all finished," Angela said, still annoyed.

"God, Angela," said Elizabeth, who was chipping off a forkful of Richard's mince pie, "are you on the rag?"

Artie's response to this unabashed inquiry was a sudden gulp that threatened to send a mixture of milk and pumpkin pie into his nose. Richard had to tap him on the back.

"No, darling," Angela said, glancing at Artie, "that comes next week." Suddenly realizing the vested interest he had in this event, Artie, while quite sure the possibility of any slip-up was remote, said a prophylactic Hail Mary.

When they had well and truly finished eating, Richard brought the meal to a close by announcing, "God, I could begin all over."

"I'm ignoring that," Angela said, reaching into her purse for a copy of *The Real Paper* and, eager to get to the business at hand, setting it on the pie-crumbed table top.

The newspaper was open to the "Personals" section of the classified ads. Angela handed Richard a red felt-tip pen and said, "Pick one, darling, and circle it."

Richard, as amenable to this command as to any other that did not require much effort, glanced at the columns advertising a cornucopia of sexual talents and needs, and more or less randomly circled the following box:

> GWM, 25, hung, good looking, seeks similar for hot times. No fats, fems, freaks or aerosol brains. Box 658.

"Your turn," Angela said, taking the red pen from Richard and handing it to Elizabeth, who dubiously scanned the lists of ecstasies and afflictions for which residents of the greater Boston area offered their blood, sweat, tears and sometimes worse.

"What's this for?" Elizabeth asked as she circled her choice:

> SBF, 35, lover of Mozart, cunnilingus and Dickens, seeks companionable gentleman willing to share her interests. Box 408.

"Don't ask so many questions," Angela replied, handing the pen to Artie. "Let's simply say it's for a good cause."

Artie, who felt embarrassed just looking at this portion of the paper, and who was afraid the waitress would see it when she came to clear the dessert plates, quickly circled the first ad he set eyes on:

> SWM, hot Latin, wishes to discipline *gringa* and rectify U.S. geopolitical crimes against the Third World. Box 255.

He pushed the paper back toward Angela and gestured for her to return it to her purse. Her response to this was to confirm their selections by reading the three circled boxes in a loud, lilting voice. He covered his ears with a napkin.

Angela, whose spirits rose with her reading, smiled for the first time that afternoon. "Oh, goodie. These all sound like charming people. I'm sure we'll be able to fulfill their requirements ever so nicely."

Artie, while he did not actually bolt from the restaurant, did push his chair backward in an instinctive movement of escape.

"Relax, darling," a by now thoroughly good-natured Angela reassured him. "It's not what you think."

"It never is," he whispered.

The others did not seek to question her further. They knew by now that she liked surprises—when, that is, she was initiating them. They would find out the results of all this in due course.

"Well, loves," she asked, as she at last folded up the paper, "what lies between here and Monday?"

Even Richard groaned at this. He and Elizabeth disgustedly rattled off the tally of deferred reading and overdue writing that awaited them: heaps of drama, jeroboams of poetry, carloads of novels, trunkfuls of criticism. "God, Angela," Elizabeth said upon concluding her list, "why'd ya have to mention it? You want me to barf my turkey? What about *you*, anyway?"

"Oh, a few little lyrics of Lovelace I thought I might brush up on," she said, reaching for her wallet.

That evening at her apartment, Artie, yellow highlighter in hand, attempted to get through as much of Thoreau's journal as he could before she called him into the bedroom to make love. While he did this, Angela watched a rerun of *Bonanza* on the enormous color set at the foot of her bed. As Artie tried to concentrate on the doings at Walden Pond, she unhelpfully kept calling out bulletins about the goings-on at the Ponderosa. "Oh, darling, I wish you would come in and watch. Little Joe is getting engaged. And you know what that means! Before the end of the hour we're going to get to see the silly female *die!*"

Suppose I just started throwing all those baskets on the floor?

In the weeks before Christmas Artie was still capable of entertaining the demons, even though by now their terror had become a bit tedious and by a certain force of will he could send them on their way. Generally, his work, in which he fell ever more behind, and Angela, about whom he felt ever more perplexed, took up most of his nervous energy, so much so that he was afraid of what would happen when he went home to the relative isolation and slow pace of Christmas vacation on Long Island. He had a bad feeling that, once the activity of the last several weeks subsided, he was going to be thrown back into his own darkest depths. He worried about a flock of mental chickens coming home to roost and his having to beat them off without Angela, without Shane and without Mrs. Crangel.

But he couldn't really think about that now, because the meeting was about to get under way. Artie was in the basement of the Freshman Union building for a "workshop" of graduate student instructors who would in the spring semester be teaching freshman composition for the first time. Ordinarily, Ph.D. candidates waited a bit longer to begin this sort of work, but one other worry Artie had these days, despite Angela's insistent patronage, was money. This was a way to earn some. It would also, he hoped, be a way of testing his vocation for teaching.

The baskets Artie was worrying over numbered about sixty. They were the means through which the freshmen communicated with their comp instructors. Across the hall from where he was sitting were about fifteen cubicles, noisy and ceilingless, where students and instructors conferred. The poor freshmen, Artie thought, getting the gist of this operation. They came to Harvard, their parents having paid a zillion dollars, and they expected to be taught by the great and the near great. Instead, for most of the first year, their only close teaching contact was with the poor and the nervous—namely, graduate students like himself. A freshman taking an ordinary program—something on the order of composition (required), introductory economics, introductory chemistry, and a low-level foreign language course—would have all his discussions conducted and grades decided not by professors (whose lectures he might hear in huge halls) but by impecunious, insecure and Ph.D.-less graduate students. Once again, Artie was glad he had gone to Brown.

The last person to enter the room was Assistant Professor Jeffrey Stanhope, who, it turned out, would be running this training session for the new instructors sitting around the table. "Hello," he said, smiling as he recognized Artie.

"Hi," said Artie.

"Teeth all fixed?" the young professor asked him, recalling their encounter at the Health Services.

"Oh, yes," said Artie, "thank you."

Jeffrey smiled, sat down and unpacked his book bag. The main business of the meeting was not so much to discuss classroom technique—an interest in teaching at Harvard being considered indicative of a lack of scholarly seriousness—but how to grade papers. The soon-to-be instructors were each handed copies of the same student essay and told to mark it up and give it a grade. The assignment was a close reading of Prince Hal's soliloquy in act 1, scene 2, of *Henry IV, Part One:*

I know you all, and will a while uphold
The unyok'd humour of your idleness;
Yet herein will I imitate the sun,
Who doth permit the base contagious clouds
To smother up his beauty from the world,
That when he please again to be himself,
Being wanted, he may be more wonder'd at,

By breaking through the foul and ugly mists
Of vapours that did seem to strangle him. . . .

Artie read through his copy and marked some faulty grammar and spelling. It didn't look too bad to him. The student seemed to understand the speech pretty well, was able to relate it to the main themes of the play and was capable of making a few adequate, if obvious, comments about the passage's imagery and meter. Artie wrote some suggestions at the bottom of the last page of the Xerox and affixed a "B–" to the essay.

When they had all finished, Jeffrey Stanhope collected the papers and tallied the grades on a blackboard:

A –	2
B+	1
B	2
B–	1
C	2
D	1

Artie was appalled. How could there be so little consensus? How could they, who were going to write dissertations interpreting things like *The Anatomy of Melancholy* and *Finnegans Wake*, not have some basic standard for something as elemental as a freshman theme? They had just made a collective idiot of themselves, he thought.

But Jeffrey, turning around from the blackboard, seemed amused. "It's not a very exact science, is it?" he said.

For the rest of the meeting he offered no fixed criteria and delivered no injunctions. He merely gave them hints: about things to flag in the margins, how much work to assign, what to talk about during conferences. Artie, who liked things to be clear—who in fact liked to take orders—was a bit bothered by all this. But he was relaxed, too. Jeffrey made him easeful. His eyes could settle on the handsome tans and blues and blonds of his head and feel rested, unthreatened. There was something kindly, intelligent and unperturbed about him. He was a bit like Richard, without the lethargy. Artie looked and listened and felt so soothed that he failed to realize that for most of the meeting Jeffrey was looking straight back at him.

When it was over, and everyone was gathering books and filing out, Jeffrey, still smiling, came up to him and said, "We never had that dinner we talked about. Remember? By the elevator in Holyoke Center?"

"Oh, right," said Artie, who did now remember, and who realized the idea had been driven from his mind by his liaison with Angela. "I guess I forgot about it. I'm sorry. I'm always forgetting things around here. I'm always going crazy with work. It's been even worse lately."

Jeffrey smiled at him. "It's likely to get worse still until exams are over next month."

"Yeah," said Artie, whose stomach tightened a little at this fresh reminder of what awaited him just after the break.

"Then why don't we have dinner the first day of the second semester? In fact, let's do it the day you teach your first class at Harvard." He took out his pocket calendar and booked the two of them for dinner on the evening of February 5, 1974. "Meet me on the steps of Warble House at five that night?"

"Okay," Artie said. Now they were both smiling over the precision with which they had fixed a date almost two months in the future.

"Good. See you."

"See you," said Artie, who felt rather happy.

The last meeting of the Symposium before Christmas seemed peculiar to Artie. During the discussion of Eliot's "Tradition and the Individual Talent," Branded, instead of offering his usual extravagant assent to all Canker said, showed signs of agitation. He kept looking around as if he expected to be caught at something; he cleared his throat and played with his tie and looked at his watch. Canker, who might have been expected to observe and resent the lack of sycophancy, didn't. Rather, he frequently broke into wide smiles during the two hours, and once or twice giggled irrelevantly. Instead of looking typically tortured and pasty, he appeared happy and high-colored. Toward the end of class, as he read a paragraph from the text, he twirled his eyeglasses in his right hand; they escaped his grip and were centrifugally carried halfway across the room. When they landed on the carpet, he cried "Oops!" and broke into a full, loud laugh.

If this unfamiliar sound added to the strangeness of the meeting, the absence of another did likewise. It took Artie a while to figure out what was missing: Little Nell's trilling and cooing. She, who never missed a class, wasn't there.

"Did you find all that a little weird today?" Artie asked Elizabeth as they walked away from Warble House with Richard and Angela.

"Yeah," she replied. "I did. Has there been some kind of lobotomy boom in the last week? Branded looked like a Watergate witness and Canker was acting like Jerry Lewis."

"And where was Little Nell?" Richard cooed.

Artie asked Angela, "How about you? Any theories?"

"Who, me? No," said Angela with a canary-swallowing look. "Couldn't possibly imagine," she said, tossing her blond hair back into the nippy winter air.

"Come on, Downing," Elizabeth said. "What's cookin'?"

"Well," said Angela, "perhaps they were . . . preoccupied?"

"With what?" Elizabeth persisted.

By way of an answer, Angela extracted from her purse the copy of *The Real Paper* whose personal ads she had had them circle at Thanksgiving dinner. She thrust it under a lamppost on Quincy Street.

"Oh, my God," whispered Artie. Elizabeth and Richard smiled.

"Okay, who'd ya send to who?" Elizabeth asked.

"Well, let's see," said Angela. "I believe I sent the 'GWM,

twenty-five, hung' and so forth to Branded; Canker got the charming black woman who likes Dickens and Mozart and cunnilingus—actually, she likes *soixante-neuf*, but the sweet thing was too shy to say it in her advert; and, oh yes, Little Nell got the aggressive Latino."

"Oh, God!" Artie exclaimed. "Is that why she was absent? We'd better check and see if she's okay!"

"Relax, darling, the GWM and SBF were both lovely persons. I talked to them on the telephone this morning."

"What did they say?" asked Richard.

"Oh, darling, I hope you don't think I asked for *details?* How tacky! I just asked for a little capsule summary. The GWM said Branded has a lot to learn, but it seems he has quite surprisingly good physical resources with which to learn it."

"What about the black chick?" Elizabeth asked.

"Well," said Angela, lilting, "she said they *tried* to chat about *Bleak House*, but they really didn't get very far. Certain things apparently got in the way of conversation. The important thing is that they both had a perfectly *lovely* time. Couldn't you tell from Canker's sweetly uncoordinated movements this afternoon?"

"But what about the Latin guy?" Artie asked, still worried. "Did he report to you this morning?"

"Well," answered Angela, "as a matter of fact he didn't."

"Oh, no!" exclaimed Artie. "How do you know Little Nell isn't bound and gagged somewhere?"

"Relax, darling," Angela said, draping an arm around him. "I'm sure she's simply a little tired."

"We've got to call her," Artie persisted.

"Oh, dear," said Angela. "Suit yourself."

They went to a phone booth near the subway kiosk in the Square. Artie got Little Nell's number from university information and dialed it.

"Hello?" said a fluting voice on the other end of the line.

Artie, suddenly timid, handed the receiver to Angela. She glared at him but didn't miss a beat.

"Hello, darling," she said, "it's Angela Downing, from the Symposium. I'm calling because I was terribly worried when I failed to see you there this afternoon."

Angela moved the receiver away from her ear and held it equidistant from the four people gathered around the phone. Little Nell's quite audible reply was not long in coming: "Oh, fear not! I am splendid. I was not there because I was accosted by one of life's magnificent surprises. These last hours I have been learning things of which most poets have failed to dream! 'Henceforth my wooing mind shall be express'd / In russet yeas and honest kersey noes . . .' " Before the line on Nell's end went dead, Artie thought he heard the sound of an honest *thwack*.

"See, love," said Angela, briskly hanging up the phone. "I'm sure it did them all a world of good."

Conundrum Hall
December 20, 1973

Dear Shane,

Because of the energy crisis, Harvard has gotten pretty stingy with the heat, and that's one more reason I'll be glad to get out of the dorm for Christmas. It's freezing. I would be spending all my time at Angela's, but when I'm there I can never be sure she won't get some idea like having pizzas delivered to all the English department faculty. In any case, she leaves Sunday for England. I'll miss her, but I'm still no nearer to understanding her than I ever was.

Here in Comus we've been going through a period of injuries. The Chinese physics student finally burned the Spanish philosophy student's hand on the latter's hot plate when they failed to resolve their argument over the vegetables and note cards, which I think I mentioned to you. Juan the janitor, who thinks we're all bizarre, and who is right, had to call security. One morning he was so put out with us that he walked up and down the corridor, ordering, "Get een your fuckeeng rooms and fuckeeng study!"

The Blue Boy was given a surprise birthday party by his boyfriend and got hurt when a boy jumped out of the cardboard cake they had in the lounge. On his way out of the cake the kid knocked over the Mad Doorknob Polisher's tea service (which he'd lent for the occasion), and Blue Boy got slightly scalded. The Hedgehog's forehead got bruised the other night, and so he's taken to wearing a boxer's sparring helmet, which he says makes things safer but decreases his chances of getting answers. And Voltears has been crying for two days over a Christmas news feature on TV about abused Canadian reindeer.

I won't be able to carry any Christmas presents home. I'll have to buy them there, because when I go down, my arms will be full of Plato, Herodotus, Melville, Hawthorne, William Dean Howells, Andrew Marvell, Wordsworth . . . I could go on. I'm more behind than ever. So is everyone else (except, of course, Angela). First semester exams are only a few weeks away and I'm frantic. Mrs. Crangel (she's the shrink) says I shouldn't overdo. I guess she thinks it's time for me to start asking the "big questions." But even when I overdo, I wind up underdone.

I'll see you in 190 days.

Signed,
Beleaguered in Boston

"Angela, I can't eat any more."

"Oh, good. Maybe we can get the waitress to yell at you. I'm told they can be very entertaining."

Artie knew that the reputation of Durgin-Park waitresses for ferocity was justified. He and Shane had been up at the Boston restaurant once after a hockey game a couple of years ago, and Shane had made the mistake of flirting with a middle-aged barracuda. He'd asked for "a side of thighs" to go with his steak. "Listen, dope fiend," she'd replied. "Button it or get it cut off."

"Who could eat all this?" Artie asked Angela, pointing to what remained on his platter of pot roast. "I mean, this would fulfill a Japanese person's protein requirements for the next six months. Maybe we could get a doggie bag."

"Darling, I'm sorry you've lost your Thanksgiving gusto, but

I would sooner mail what's there to Japan than walk it home in some dripping bag to a dog we don't own. Let's just pay up."

As they did, Angela made comfortable banter with the waitress. Artie noticed, not for the first time, how well she got on with these women who waited tables or cleaned the offices in Warble House. He lately had got a more precise idea of her feelings toward her own sex. What she liked, it seemed, were the idle rich and the working poor. The only ones she had no time for were women like herself—educated professionals. In Elizabeth's case, the truck-driver's diction seemed to allow for an exception.

It was the last Saturday before Christmas and Artie was in a bad humor, irritated by Angela's unconcern over work as his own anxiety about papers and exams mounted. He certainly hadn't wanted to spend time on another shopping spree, which was what they were on. But Angela had pouted: "Not even for presents for me to take home? Little bundles for Britain, where Teddy Heath is only permitting us to heat a single room in each house? Where two Christmas shopping days have been cancelled? Where there isn't even going to be any telly after ten-thirty—all because of these bloody Arabs and coal miners?" She said she wanted to get particularly American gifts ("little tins of maple syrup, submachine guns, that sort of thing") and needed his advice. Durgin-Park had been proposed as another bit of folk experience, and Artie felt patriotically obliged to comply.

Still, he was grumpy, and, driving back to Cambridge, they kept getting into arguments. When, for example, they stopped short at a light and he could hear the extra gasoline sloshing in the trunk, he complained, "You know, they say one gallon of that stuff equals fourteen sticks of dynamite."

"Oh, relax. It's all right as long as you don't swallow it."

Artie was puzzled.

"The gasoline, sweetie. People have been siphoning it from one car to another. They get the action going with a little suck."

"God," Artie said.

"A bit like Linda Lovelace. Wonderful about that award, don't you think?" The star of *Deep Throat* had recently been given the *Harvard Lampoon*'s "Wilde Oscar."

"Can't you think about anything else?"

"You mean sex?"

"Yes."

"I might ask why you can't seem to think about it a little more."

Silence followed, during which Artie wondered why his ardor had recently diminished. He put it down to the pressure of work, but he knew it was something else, too—a fear that he was becoming Angela's creature, that he couldn't make a move without her approval. He was worried about being spellbound by a woman he still really couldn't claim to know. Tonight he would give her his modest Christmas present, a coffee-table book called *Mysterious Britain*. Coals to Newcastle, he thought now, or more like enigmas to Stonehenge.

They walked through Harvard Square without speaking. Some Salvation Army members made tired tootlings outside the Coop, where they were headed for one last present for a cousin of Angela's. Artie shuffled sullenly along, looking at his shoes, until he heard a Texas accent say, "Well, look who it is. What are you two up to?"

It was Mrs. Crangel, relaxed and gangly in her unbuttoned maxi coat, walking beside a lean, tall man in a reindeer sweater whom she introduced as her husband. Artie had perked up and given a big grin at the sight of her, and Angela had immediately noticed. She answered Mrs. Crangel's question for him: "I shouldn't think you'd need to ask what we're 'up to.' Surely you hear all about what we do when he shows up for your little . . . sessions?"

"We talk about a lot of things," Mrs. Crangel replied in a neutral drawl.

"That's just fine," Angela said, propelling Artie forward by the elbow. "But do remember: I'm in charge now."

Artie couldn't believe this. The Crangels were walking away. Angela kept pushing him forward. He looked back over his shoulder, intending to apologize to Mrs. Crangel, expecting a look of therapeutic reassurance. He caught her eye.

"What a *bitch*," Mrs. Crangel called out.

11

At 2:30 A.M., having returned from midnight Mass with his parents, Artie was up in his room at work on a tangled outline for an end-of-term paper, on Donne's *Metempsychosis*, for Herman Howell. Only Artie, Shane might have noted, could pull an all-nighter on Christmas Eve. Books were all around his room, taking up chairs, resting on slippers, crowding plants.

He had brought more than his arms could carry when he came to Long Island the other day. Getting out of the Port Authority terminal, he slid in some slush, and volumes of Plato, Herbert and Hawthorne went sliding into the Eighth Avenue gutter. A hooker with orange hair and a microskirt helped retrieve them.

Artie now wondered if Widener Library would fine him for the water-warped books. This concern mixed itself with others: that he would never get the Donne paper finished on time, that he was three weeks behind in reading for the American literature summary, and that the little Greek he knew was leaking hour by hour from his brain—he would be surprised if there was anything left by the exam.

He felt worse than he had since late October. His parents had looked at him with worried faces in church earlier. He felt guilty: he had not given them any indication of his troubles these last months. His letters and calls home had been cheerful fakes. He'd thought he was protecting them. Actually, he was underestimating them, and he knew it. Kind and shrewd, they would have been able to rise to the occasion of his distress had he let them. Sensing that distress in church, they felt more excluded than shielded. But even so, thought Artie, how could he make them understand? They wanted Harvard so badly for their only child; how could he tell them he thought about leaving it three times a day?

They had opened their presents before Mass. His, from them, was a briefcase.

"Artie, get up, you've got a phone call. From England. It's a girl."

What girl? Artie thought, rising from the chair in which he'd fallen asleep. It was 8:00 Christmas morning.

"Well, hello, love! Merry Christmas! Your father is charming. We chatted for a bit before I asked him where you were. He replied 'Neither here nor there.' What a shame the family humor genes were lost after him."

Angela's accent woke him up like a slap of after-shave. To his father, Artie realized, Angela *was* a girl. But he had as much trouble thinking of her as a girl as he did of himself as a man.

She seemed in wonderful spirits. She was in Cambridge, at her ex-lover's, about to sit down to Christmas dinner. Her ex-husband was with them. Artie thought he should feel jealous, but what he mostly felt was unreal.

Angela lilted joyfully over the ocean. "Oh, darling! The wools! The tweeds! The cashmeres! We're a bit low on the old fuel, but the shops are simply marvelous. I've bought one of everything."

Artie asked her how long she would be staying with her ex-lover.

"Oh, not long. I'm just stopping here on my way out to see my spinster aunt in Madingley. I'm going to read to her and walk her dog for the next week or so. Then I'm off to my parents'."

Even though Artie's credulity in romantic matters had not been strained by much experience, he couldn't bring himself to believe this itinerary.

"Now, darling, you'll never guess from whom I received the most wonderful Christmas telegram. I won't even let you try, as it will run up poor Christopher's bill. It was from Little Nell! 'Gone to Panama for sudden nuptials' was how she put it. 'Felt you must know, because you were the first whose words I heard after feeling the warmth of Rodrigo.' I must say I admire her: no skimping on the old articles and prepositions just to save a few pence. Anyway, I think it's *marvelous*. See what good I can do when I try? I daresay, with Rodrigo's proclivities the dear thing will never require blush-on again.

"Now, darling, I'm not coming back until later than the last minute, February fifth or some such date. I'm writing to tell Monsieur Dubois that I have influenza and can't possibly make the examination in medieval French on the fourteenth of January. It's my only one. I'll just dash off a make-up when I get back. Now, before I hang up, sweet, how are you?"

December 26, 1973

Dear Mrs. Crangel,

I know we thought I wasn't going to be back for a while, but I think I'm going to have to return to Harvard right after New Year's, because I still have more work than I can easily handle with the library down here. I'm going to drop by your office on the 5th. Don't come in on account of me, but there are really some things I'd like to talk about if you're around.

Sincerely,
Arthur Dunne

P.S. I'm really sorry about last Saturday in the Square.

Artie sat on the top row of frozen bleachers near the football field of M. Scott Carpenter High School. He was not recalling past gridiron glories; he was remembering upset stomachs during gym. He had an upset stomach now, a stomach as upset as it had been through most of October. Eating was once more difficult, and he only made a show of it for his mother. One good thing about going back to Harvard tomorrow would be no longer having to fake gusto at the table.

He let the cold air rip through him. His reserves of optimism were at a two-month low. The whole fall, in fact everything since Brown, had begun to seem like something someone had made up: Harvard, Canker, Angela, his work—even Mrs. Crangel. He had just come from the local public library, where he had had the most protracted attack of the demons in weeks. He had imagined the consequences of hurling several Dewey decimal points' worth of books over the mezzanine rail and into the children's section.

A gust of wind blew against the left side of his face. He longed for Shane and wondered if he was longing for Angela. He knew he was jealous of her ex-lover and her ex-husband, of all the people she was with instead of him. But was he really missing her? She was so much a part of the unreality of the last several months that missing her now seemed beside the point. It would be like missing Disneyland. He had wonderful memories of the day he spent there with his cousins in 1962, but it wasn't something you could really miss.

He closed his eyes. It was January 2, 1974, and he was, he believed, back to square one.

John Donne's *Metempsychosis*, Artie knew, has to do with the transmigration of the soul. He also knew that his own soul wasn't going anywhere. In fact, he wondered if it was even still alive, so long had it gone unwatered by any Keatsian reflections upon finer things. He was back at his desk in Comus, eating dried apricots and trying to bang out his paper for Herman Howell. He had no special fondness for dried apricots; they were just one of six items he had earlier that evening thrown almost randomly into his cart during a ten-minute run to the Evergood Market, the only break he was going to allow himself today.

Comus remained nearly empty. It would be a few days before

people drifted back for the reading period, those couple of weeks built into each semester of the Harvard calendar, days that in the months before Christmas seemed filled with the possibility of catching up on all one's undone reading, and now, as they actually came around, seemed hopelessly short. Artie was doing his best to work, but the paper just wouldn't come.

He realized that this had something to do with the fact that most of those residents whose weird movements and utterances had so agitated him all term were still away. Just as rural migrants to Manhattan eventually can't sleep without the noise of traffic, Artie had come to depend on the clamor in the corridor for his natural aural environment. Now the Hedgehog and Voltears were away. No slamming or weeping could be heard in the hall. The only sounds outside his door were being made by the Mad Doorknob Polisher, who, time on his spotless hands, was burnishing all the switch plates and name-card holders on the hall, *gratis*. Earlier in the day Artie had spotted the Gainsborough boy, whose burned hand was now healed, rigging up a sort of jungle swing in his room—presumably a more exciting replacement for the broken dorm chair. But otherwise he too was silent these days, keeping a low, if still pretty, profile.

By 10:30 Artie was only on page six of what was supposed to be a twenty-page paper. If he didn't complete it tomorrow, doing the work he had left for his other courses, especially Greek, would be out of the question. But he could no longer think, and when Freddie came bursting into his room, he was glad of the distraction.

For all the punishing rigor attributed to the law school, Freddie still looked a model of grooming and fresh energy, capable of the last thing Artie could find in his own psychological repertoire—spontaneity.

"Hey, Art," he said, "c'mon. I just got a phony AT&T credit card. Let's call up everyone we ever met. Have you got Shane's number in California? Let's buzz him and talk all night."

More potential guilt, thought Artie, who had never liked the light-fingeredness of his fellow undergraduates in the Vietnam days, when to snatch a book from the university bookstore was to "liberate" it from the corporate establishment, and to swindle some gas out of the local Texaco operator was to "obtain reparations from the military-industrial complex." Still, it wasn't exactly *his* phony credit card they were talking about, and the thought of speaking to Shane was buoying. Perhaps, he thought, life with Angela was inuring him to these ethical dilemmas. He got up from his chair and went with Freddie, who had his own phone, to the law school.

"Ah, shit," said Freddie, after reaching California. "His brother says he's out somewhere. He won't be back tonight. Who else can we call?"

Artie, for no more than a second, thought about trying to reach Angela. But going from a domestic to a transatlantic ripoff seemed like upping the ante of sinfulness from venial to mortal. Besides, he wasn't sure how she'd react. So he just shrugged his shoulders in reply to Freddie.

"Come on, we gotta call *somebody*. We can't let this card go to waste. Tomorrow I've got to give it back to its rightful owner. Hey, how about Boodie?"

A moment later they were talking to Providence.

"Hey, Boodie! It's your old friends Freddie and Art!"

There was a pause on the other end before Boodie's spooky voice complained, "Yooo shouldn't dooo this. It disrupts my beta waves if I have to get up in the middle of the night."

"Aw, Bood," protested Freddie. "It's only one-thirty. Hey, how's Juniper? Yank his tail. Make him say hi."

"Freddie," Boodie responded, his vowels rising and falling like wind in a cemetery, "yooo and Artie should go to bed. I don't know what's wrong with all of yooo. Last week Shane called me at five A.M. He seemed very odd."

"He must have forgotten the time difference," Freddie explained. "It would only have been two in California."

Artie was curious. Why would Shane have called Boodie? He put this question to him.

"Because," explained Boodie, "he wanted to know if he'd left an amplifier in the basement when he moooved out last spring." Shane, while at Brown, had sporadically been lead guitarist and singer for a heavy-metal band called the Nocturnal Emissions. "I told him there was nothing here."

Artie let Freddie do the rest of the talking. Shane's sudden interest in his amplifier, and what Boodie said about his sounding odd—no mean statement, coming from Boodie—bothered him a little. A few minutes later he said good-bye to Freddie and headed back to Comus, determined to write Shane a letter asking what was up and then pull an all-nighter on the Donne paper.

When he arrived back on the third floor, at 2 A.M., things were less sepulchral than they had been earlier. In fact, there was a belated New Year's party taking place among the few available residents down the hall. As Artie unlocked his door, the Gainsborough boy, carrying a bottle and a glass, came into the corridor and asked, "A little champagne, Artie? Just a splash?"

He was clad only in a white sash with 1974 written on it.

Artie declined.

It was, in fact, to Angela that he wound up writing:

Comus Hall
January 4, 1974

Dear Angela,

When you called my folks' house, you didn't give me much of a chance to tell you how I was. So I'll elaborate a little on my misery. I'm back in this loony place trying to work on Donne for Howell. And I'm not making much progress. (Are you mailing your paper to him? It's due way before you say you're coming back.)

Yesterday afternoon I had hot chocolate with Elizabeth at

Brigham's. I was moping around and I guess she noticed, because she said, "Lemme guess. You're missing Mam'zelle Gotrocks." (A reference to you.) I told her what I'll tell you—i.e., the truth—i.e., yes. Why are you staying away so long? Who are you with? (Harvard English department translation: With whom are you?) Who do you want to be with more than me?

Do you miss me? You say you're "in charge" of me. Does that entail missing me, or are you happy to be on vacation from your social work—i.e., me? I don't know anything about how you feel about me. I don't know anything about you. Come home. Tell me. Talk to me. Hold me. Kiss me. Love me.

Love you,
Artie

The following morning Artie dropped in on Mrs. Crangel, who was wearing blue jeans and sneakers and an orange University of Texas sweatshirt.

"I don't know. I mean, sometimes I think I'm as bad off as ever. Like with the demons. I've been having them almost as much as back in October. Even at midnight Mass on Christmas, I kept wondering about things like, what if I just grabbed the collection basket and dumped it in the holy water? And now that I'm back here, I'm so scared of work and exams I can hardly eat again. Even Shane seems weird. My friend Freddie and I couldn't get hold of him on the phone, and what we heard about him doesn't sound right."

"Maybe," Mrs. Crangel said, smiling, "this could all just be a temporary setback? Even we 'normal' people have our ups and downs."

"I hope so," said Artie.

"What do you hear from Angela?"

"She's not coming back until the beginning of next month."

"Miss her?"

"Yes," Artie said automatically, before adding, "No. Both. I mean, I just wrote and told her I miss her, and I do miss the excitement and the, you know . . ."

"The sex," Mrs. Crangel said.

"Yes," said Artie, eager to move on from this. "But how can I really miss her if she won't miss me?"

"And you don't think she does?" Mrs. Crangel asked.

"I don't know," Artie said.

"Do you think you love her?"

"I don't know," Artie repeated.

"Is it time to ask yourself if you do? How long has it been? Two months?"

"I guess it's time," said Artie. "But who has time for anything?" he almost shouted. "I'm only on page nine of my *Metempsychosis* paper!"

Mrs. Crangel persisted. "Let's say you don't love her? Would that be so terrible?"

"But shouldn't we love one another? Doing what we, you know, after all, keep doing?"

"Maybe in an ideal world," Mrs. Crangel answered. "Not necessarily in this one."

Artie was stymied. He shrugged his shoulders and smiled apologetically. He played with his shoelace and looked at the rug.

"Do you really think she's a bitch?" he asked.

"Hour's up," said Mrs. Crangel.

A few weeks later Artie learned that he had passed all his courses with nothing lower than a B-plus in Greek. He received the news with exhausted disbelief. The *Metempsychosis* paper had been praised by Herman Howell: "Slightly less jaunty than your earlier, shorter efforts, but a commodious and informed appraisal nonetheless." His "take-home" exam for the Symposium had been given an A-minus and a few cursory check marks. (Artie suspected that Canker hadn't read the exams at all, and that Branded had been the one to exert himself over the ticks; in fact, everyone received an A-minus.) The Greek exam had been the most trying. Artie had attempted to memorize all the sentences in the text in English, hoping he could recognize enough key words when he saw the Greek to call up the rest from memory. On the whole this strategy worked well, though he did mangle some of the textbook's descriptions of treacherous women and valiant warriors, which resulted in some peculiar outfits walking around Ilion.

The only surprising moment during exams came in the Houghton Reading Room, when the German woman passed out the books for which the students in the director's seminar were to write up on-the-spot bibliographical descriptions. When she put an early-eighteenth-century edition of *Areopagitica* before Artie, she whispered, "Iss good thing iss not T. S. Eliot, no?" and walked away giggling after poking him in the ribs.

The semester ended, and Artie slept deeply during the several days of intersession.

"You live in Pennypacker, don't you?" a red-headed boy from Michigan asked Artie.

"No. I'm the teacher," he responded. They were seated at a large table in a room in the Freshman Union building, waiting for the rest of the composition class to arrive.

"You're kidding," said the boy from Michigan, good-naturedly.

Except for a few gray hairs at his right temple, Artie did look young enough to be a freshman, and he now decided that it might be a good idea, for purposes of identification and authority, if he stood near the blackboard while the rest of the students came in. He also wrote his name on it: ARTHUR DUNNE, in capital letters he wished were less blocky and childish looking. As the rest of the class ambled in—the usual Harvard roomful of valedictorians from New York and Massachusetts and Ohio and California, and what Angela would have called East Dakota, all of them slowly getting used to a new ratio of their size as fish relative to that of the pond—Artie wondered if he was going to be able to go through with it. Ever since high school he had thought he would like to spend his life talking about books, but now that he was about to start doing that—and even get paid for it—he was afraid he wasn't going to pull it off.

"Hi. I'm Artie Dunne. This is freshman composition. You're the students." The last of these sentences just tumbled inanely out, as if Artie were so desperate to get the lay of the land in this particular brave new world that he was recording every rock and mound in sight. The students thought he was making a sort of small friendly joke. They laughed, and to Artie's surprise the ice was broken.

He had decided that their first assignment was going to be a two-page explication of the poem "Man and Wife," by the Harvard English department's magnificent part-time asset, Robert Lowell. Looking at his notes, Artie briefly explained Lowell's career and the place of *Life Studies* in the history of recent American poetry. Every so often he would write a name or a date on the blackboard, less from pedagogical necessity than the nervous sense that this was what he was supposed to do.

The future humanities majors did not copy down what he wrote; to them composition was just a required course, a sort of exhibition game they had to dawdle through in freshman year. But the pre-meds, for whom every course meant a crucial grade, looked at the blackboard as if they might inhale the chalked words right off the slate. Like court reporters, they took down everything Artie said.

But they were a minority, and by the time ten minutes had passed, Artie sensed he was losing the rest of them with his overprepared lecture. Remembering something Jeffrey Stanhope had said at their meeting last month, he decided it was time to make them "participate."

"Why don't you read through the poem in front of you now,

so we can start discussing what *you* think it means," he instructed, shifting gears quickly enough to surprise even some of the bored humanities majors.

As the students silently read their dittoed sheets, Artie realized that he had nothing to do. So he retied one of his shoes, shuffled through his notes and combed his hair with his hands. So abstracted did he now feel from the class that, while most of them were reading the last stanza, he began, unaware of what he was doing, to hum.

A large girl from Maine glared at him as if he were a moron.

"Sorry," he said.

"Don't mention it," she replied, returning her attention to the poem.

In elementary school the custom was for students to put their heads down when they had completed whatever silent reading or test taking the class was engaged in. Artie thought asking these students to do that might be a gauche move, so he just waited for several pairs of eyes to come up from the dittos.

"Okay, then," he said, like a peppy Little League coach who asks to hear a little chatter in the outfield, "what's going on in this poem?"

There was no response. Artie framed his question more precisely: "What has happened to this marriage? The speaker makes reference to the days in which he first got to know his wife, years ago. What's happened in the intervening time?"

For another moment, more silence. Then a very small boy, who really did look younger than Artie, and whose thick glasses gave him the appearance of the child genius in Walt Disney movies, raised his hand. Artie nodded to him.

"I believe," the small boy said, "that it is primarily Mrs. Lowell's dispositional alteration which is responsible for the celerity with which their love has atrophied."

Artie stared at him. Something in the back of his critical mind told him he should be saying something about how even in a so-called confessional poem like this one, we should be wary of identifying the speaker with the real-life poet, but he was frozen before the kid's impassive face and architectonic diction. Several seconds passed before he could fulfill his professional duty to respond, and then all he could manage to say was "What's your name?"

"Adam Bukovsky."

"Thank you," Artie said after another pause. Aware that he had to bring the class down to less dizzying rhetorical heights, and worried that the rest of the students might get the idea he was less smart than Bukovsky, he moved quickly to another question on his list of notes. "In what sense," he asked, "could the wife in this poem be considered a kind of heroine?"

Bukovsky fortunately did not raise his hand. Instead, one of the pre-meds put his high in the air. Artie called on him.

"Because maybe she's sort of like a drug, you know, that he's sort of addicted to her, like one can get to heroin?"

Artie nodded consideringly. Clearly there was a wide range of critical ability in this room. Relieved not to be stuck with a class full of Bukovskys, he said, "Uh, yes, that's interesting. Anyone else?"

And to his surprise there *was* someone else. And then someone else. Pretty soon the class was rolling along through an energetic discussion of the poem's particulars, its ironies, its mixed diction, its 1950s atmosphere—the works. And Artie discovered he was rather good at guiding the voices before him in productive enterprise. He would explain to them some of the poem's knottier lines—who, for example, the Rahvs were; what a "climacteric" was (even Bukovsky didn't seem quite sure of that)—and let them take it from there. As the end of the hour approached, only one student hadn't entered the discussion. Artie, not wanting to press her but wanting to make sure she got her inning, smiled at her and asked, "How about you? Any judgments to make about Robert Lowell before we wind up?"

The girl paused for a second before saying, "I was standing on line behind him yesterday at Harvard Trust. He borrowed my pen. He seemed real nice."

One of the pre-meds made a note of this.

Then the bell rang, and Artie left the Union building feeling unexpectedly high. He could, he realized, get to like this, which was not an unpleasant feeling to have about what was likely to be his life's work.

He went back to Comus to pick up his mail before going to meet Jeffrey Stanhope on the steps of Warble House.

On the back of a large postcard depicting a Victorian cartoonist's idea of Jack the Ripper, he read the following:

London
January 27, 1974

Sweetie,

Thanks for yours of New Year's Day plus three. I am at a counter in Fortnum & Mason, surrounded by lots of prosperous grannies. It's a cozy sight, takes the chill off what over here we're calling "the winter of our discontent." (Hope you know that line. It's *sure* to be on the M.A. tests. Studying hard?) I'm off to meet a friend at the National Gallery to do a little spin round our past glories — small comfort as we continue our rapid drive to replicate Rumania.

You do ask rather a lot of questions in your letter.

Angela

Not even "Love." Just "Angela." With all the "sweeties" and brittle-bright stuff she lavished on everyone. Not the answer to a single question; just an order not to ask them. It would of course have been too much for her to tell him who the friend she was meeting was. Just as it would have been too much to send a letter instead of a postcard. He had waited a month for this. She didn't even say when she would bother to show up for the second

y seemed to find it, or perhaps the manner in which it was
›sed, of considerable interest.

ie kept eating and drinking. After a fourth glass of wine he
d and said, "Gosh, I've told you my whole life story"—
s such things as the demons and Angela, he might have
—"and I haven't given you a chance to say anything."

frey, whose blue eyes indicated that he would much rather
listening, consented to give a condensed version of his own
y, which he turned into a sort of upscale parody of *David
erfield*. Instead of Murdstone and Grinby there had been
r, Yale, a Rhodes scholarship, and then Yale again. He
een born of prosperous and successful academics and would
nue their ways—although probably not at Harvard, which
a point of almost never granting tenure from the ranks. He
d wind up at a place like Williams or Smith, "mildly suc-
il and an 'ornament' to the English department." He had
y his own admission, "a charmed life, a golden kid's. When
eleven I got my own skis. When I was thirteen I got taken
rope. When I was seventeen I got a car. The only thing
ver had by the age of eighteen was a zit."

ie, whose shyness of human exudings was extreme, man-
to find this very funny, and he was drunk enough that it
him a full twenty seconds to stop laughing. Jeffrey did not
natters when, as he walked over to the television, he tickled
"Let's check the news," he said. It was eleven o'clock.

kay," said Artie, recovering.

ey both expected the usual rundown of pre-impeachment
s by the House Judiciary Committee. But tonight the main
was that the granddaughter of William Randolph Hearst
been kidnapped from her apartment in Berkeley by some
ularly unappealing radicals who were making some unusu-
topian ransom demands.

ie could tell that the newsman wasn't sure whether this story
upposed to be ludicrous or frightening. But he didn't find

semester. God forbid she should ask him to meet her plane. Maybe she wouldn't come back at all.

Well, let her stay in New Rumania. He was sick of being pampered and swatted and ignored and tyrannized. Now he knew what he meant to her. Nothing. He was a little diversion, a project, and she was obviously getting tired of him.

He stuffed the postcard into his copy of *Life Studies* and walked out of the dorm. In the Square he stopped in front of the window of the Paperback Booksmith and spent a minute looking through his reflection to a stack of copies of *How to Be Your Own Best Friend*.

That's what he would be, he decided, revving himself into false gaiety as he turned toward Quincy Street to meet Jeffrey. He would be his own best friend.

"And for a while I thought, oh boy, I'm never going to get through this—especially when I heard this Bukovsky kid's answer—but a little after that things picked up, and I sort of couldn't believe it but I had this sudden feeling that things were going well, and I could almost hear myself talking, from outside myself, you know? And I didn't even sound stupid—not by the end of the hour, anyway—and they kept talking really excitedly about the poem."

Jeffrey Stanhope was smiling as he listened to Artie, who was talking with the sort of breathlessness he usually demonstrated around Shane. With the genuine euphoria left over from class, and the false euphoria of his anti-Angelan determination, Artie was not paying much attention to the traffic, and Jeffrey had to pull him back by the elbow when he nearly walked in front of an Oldsmobile near the Gulf station on Mass. Ave. They were on their way to Jeffrey's apartment in Bradford House, where he was a tutor—a position that, like the house system itself, owed its existence to Harvard's halfhearted aping of the Oxbridge college model.

Jeffrey was going to cook their long-planned dinner. This, he said, would be better than fighting the crowds of students sure to be at the Blue Parrot or Natalie's because they were unable to face dormitory food on the first night of the new semester.

"So you think you'll like teaching," Jeffrey summed up, smiling, as they walked into the lobby of Bradford, a modern high-rise that, despite its fancy European architect, still looked like a thousand other dormitories put up during the Great Society years.

"I think I might," Artie responded.

"Hi, Jeff!" A healthy-looking blond girl coming back from a run waved as Jeffrey and Artie got into the elevator. Her warm-up suit was sweated through, and it stuck to the middle regions of her body with wonderful suggestions of contour.

"One of my tutees," Jeffrey explained to Artie.

He opened the door to his top-floor apartment.

"Gee," said Artie. "This is really nice." Through the huge windows he could see the lights of Boston and the shimmering Charles. The riverscape appeared perfect. It was dark enough so that he couldn't see the plywood panels that patched over the fallen glass of the ill-fated new John Hancock building.

The next sounds Artie heard, as he continued to admire the view, were those of a Jackson Browne album. This surprised him. Although Jeffrey could hardly have been more than thirty, Artie would have predicted something, well, a little less groovy, a little more likely to be found on a music syllabus. Artie, whose ignorance of music composed before 1965 was profound, was pleased. He was crazy about Jackson Browne, whom Shane had once described as "a screwed-up little guy, just like you, Urn Man."

"What do you want to drink?" Jeffrey called from the kitchen.

"Oh, anything is fine," Artie replied.

"That's not helpful," Jeffrey sing-songed.

Artie laughed. "Do you have beer?"

"Heineken okay?"

"That's fine. Thanks." Artie, whose social skills were embry-

onic, had a notion that there was someth
asking for beer before dinner. Perhaps he
a vodka collins or a glass of white wine
what he wanted, and something told hi
out of his way to look all right to Jeffrey,
was.

"I'm going to get this stuff started," Jef
a pot onto the stove. "I'll come out and

In the midst of the pot's bubbling and
choppings and shreddings, other noise ros
the parking lot twelve floors below. With
aged to make it out. It was a chant that kep

"Free Patty! Free Patty!" some prosper
alienated-looking students were shouting

"Do you know what that's about?" Artie

"Probably some friend of theirs who's
for lousy first-term grades," Jeffrey surmi

When Jeffrey brought in the plates wit
dinner, which was prepared with an ap
casualness and imagination, Artie was in
on a salad dressing bottle. "Sorry," he sa
everything these days. It's kind of a nervo
there's going to be a test."

Artie wound up eating plenty, an in
laxed. In any case, Jeffrey didn't seem th
as Shane might, or to break his spine
posture, as Angela sometimes threaten
drank, the more prodigal his words bec
and on, and Jeffrey, who never stopped s
to hear more and more of them. By 9
automatic for some time and had comn
tobiographical details ranging from his
Shakespeare to the time he got stung by
single day. Artie knew his life so far had

it funny at all. Some enormity in it touched him immediately. Patricia Hearst's life couldn't be more remote from his, but what he imagined happening to her right now summoned back all his fears of disaster and contingency. His heart beat faster and his face went white. Before the broadcast went to another story, he asked for another glass of wine and put his hands in his pockets.

Jeffrey watched him.

"God," Artie said. "Maybe it's easier to be a scholarship kid than a golden kid." He smiled weakly.

Jeffrey got up, turned off the television, and returned to the couch.

"I don't think you think anything's easy, do you?" he whispered to Artie.

Artie, really very drunk now, shook his head no.

"You're wrong," Jeffrey whispered, reaching across the couch and taking him in his arms. "Being here with you is."

Artie said nothing.

Jeffrey whispered, "Some golden kids are lonely."

"Really?" Artie asked, looking up.

Jeffrey nodded yes and closed his blue eyes for the first time that evening. "Stay here tonight," he said to Artie.

At 11:12 P.M. Jeffrey Stanhope turned out the lights in Bradford C-12A. Had Artie looked out the window at that moment, he might have seen the plane that, a few hours late out of New York, was bringing Angela Downing back to Logan Airport and the spring semester at Harvard.

12

The wine Artie had been drinking until eleven o'clock was red, and the racing heart he awoke with at 4 A.M. was from both gastronomical and emotional tumult. Jeffrey Stanhope slept on beside him, his breathing making his blond aureole of hair vibrate ever so slightly as Artie tried to grapple with the question of What He Had Done.

He didn't get very far. Everything in his upbringing told him to be repelled by the carnal part of it, but he was not. He doubted this was something he was going to make an erotic career of, but it had been tender and exciting. In fact, all he could find to feel guilty about, as his hangover began to gather, was that he wasn't more disgusted with himself.

If it had been less overwhelming than what went on between him and Angela, it was different in another way as well. When Jeffrey held him, he paid *attention* to him. When Angela held him, she might keep up a spectacular flow of instructions and endearments, but her real awareness always seemed elsewhere, perhaps in the episode of *Kojak* she'd just seen, maybe in a sweater shop near the Magdalene Bridge. Being the object of someone's undivided regard was a pleasant novelty.

Jeffrey might have been protective and sheltering in the way most of Artie's friends and bed mates had been in the past, but Artie realized that in some odd way he himself had been in charge of what went on here, that Jeffrey needed someone—enough to have conceived a desire for him on the basis of a few encounters where he had been no more than his cute, bumbling self. Jeffrey Stanhope really *was* a lonely golden kid; that hadn't been just a line. And he somehow thought Artie could help him. By letting himself—Artie—be protected by him—Jeffrey—he made Jeffrey feel better. To Artie's knowledge, no one had ever been dependent on him, even inversely, and the thought that someone might imagine himself to be was worrying. *It's not possible*, he thought. *I'm not up to it.* His self-esteem was too low.

But maybe that was how you developed self-esteem: from someone else's need of you. Maybe a subconscious awareness of this was his own motive for getting into Jeffrey's bed. Maybe he and Jeffrey were really playing the same game, a *folie à deux*.

Or maybe, subconsciously, he was dumping Angela before she could dump him.

Maybe he'd just been drunk.

Until about 7 A.M. Artie turned these possibilities over and over in what Shane had once called "that fucking little blender you've got for a head." Then the telephone in the living room rang.

He had a quick decision to make: to take the one-in-a-million chance, if he answered it, that someone would recognize his voice and figure out what had happened, or to wake Jeffrey, thereby hastening the postcoital postmortem he was dreading.

He chose the former course, padding silently into the next room and whispering, macho style, into the phone, "Hello?"

A familiar sound lilted through the receiver. "Well, love! You seem all moved in. And how was it? Exquisite? Rockets? Cymbals? Fireworks on the beach?"

How . . .

Angela went on. "Oh, love, one didn't have to be a genius. After I called your gruesome dormitory at midnight and you weren't in, I called round to Richard and Elizabeth, who told me you were supposed to be dining with Massachusetts' answer to Rupert Brooke. That's when I recalled the afternoon just before the vac when you and I ran into your new beau in the Yard. Remember? The two of you happily confirming your first-day-of-term dinner plans? Even then something about the twinkle in the young prof's eye gave me the feeling *you* were going to be the postprandial mint. Well, love, I must say, you could do worse. He's *quite* cute. *Wonderful* ears."

"Please, Angela," Artie whispered, scared that Jeffrey would awaken. "Don't make this worse for me. I feel awful. I don't know how I'm ever going to get my head straightened out after this."

"Straightening out your head, love, strikes me as labor roughly comparable to cleansing the Augean stables."

Artie's public school education had not prepared him to recognize many classical allusions, but he could get the drift of this one. He said nothing. Angela continued on without him, "Well, darling, it's really not *so* bad. Not if you compare it to October. As Elizabeth might put it: better your hands should be on Stanhope than in your pockets." Actually, Artie realized, she was echoing Mrs. Crangel. "If you want to go back to the Herculean image," Angela went on, her voice showing signs of the gentleness of which she was fleetingly capable, "at least this shit is real."

It was small consolation, but he knew what she meant.

The postmortem Artie feared never took place, because after getting off the phone with Angela, he went back into the bedroom, put on his clothes and sneaked out of Bradford C-12A without waking Jeffrey. He knew it was a rotten thing to do.

He went off to his first new course of the semester, a required one in the history and structure of the English language. By the middle of the opening lecture, which paid attention to such phenomena as the great vowel shift and umlaut and ablaut and other things that sounded like German traffic signs, he felt sure he was locked into yet another subject for which he had no facility.

In the late afternoon he barricaded himself in Comus. He was alarmed by having begun a second affair in three months, right in the middle of new assaults of work and the demons. He felt a need to touch base with his past, a need that expressed itself in a postcard to Shane:

> I've called you a couple of times but your brother never knows where you are and sounds really angry. Did you get my last letter? I mentioned that Boodie says (*Boodie* says!) you sounded peculiar when you called him about your amplifier. Is anything wrong? I'm sort of worried. (*I'm* sort of worried about *you!*)
>
> Artie

He *was* worried, sort of, mostly out of fear that Shane would become too indisposed to help him with his own never-ending problems and alarms. At this moment he would have liked to have him available to listen to all the conflicting emotions his encounter with Jeffrey Stanhope was putting into play inside his head. But if Shane were actually here, could he really tell him about it? "Gee, Urn Man, I don't know. A *guy?*" he could imagine him saying. "The real JK never went in for that shit. Why don't you leave that to all those 1890s fruits?" And maybe he'd be right. The more Artie thought about it that day, the more he began to dread telling Mrs. Crangel about it. Yet he couldn't in good conscience leave it out. That would be like omitting the biggest sin of the week when one went to Saturday confession.

Artie had no idea what his romantic or sexual status was now. Was he still Angela's lover? Was he Jeffrey's? Both? Neither? Why had fortune suddenly thrust him—a pygmy among paragons—into their beds? His objective analysis of the situation was further impeded, on his way back upstairs from mailing the postcard, by a laughing shriek coming from the Gainsborough boy's room: "No! Don't! You'll break the *rope!*" God, was he one of *them* now?

Artie knew that in order to get their best effects, poets less gifted than Keats usually needed to simplify, not multiply, their images and sounds and rhythms. He felt less gifted than anyone he knew at merely living life, and so he decided that simplification had to be the order of his day. He couldn't, he *knew* he couldn't, carry on with Jeffrey Stanhope, whatever comforts and rewards there might be in being cared about in that way. If he continued to have two affairs—both of them morally dubious—at the same time he attempted to cope with school, he would probably be trying to stick his feet inside his pockets, along with his hands, before another week went by.

He picked up the phone and did what he had to do.

"Hello?" said Jeffrey on the other end.

"Hi," said Artie.

"Artie, I've been worried about you."

"I'm sorry. I didn't mean to leave in such a rush. It's just that, well, I mean, I guess I should say that, well, I don't think I, uh, can see you again."

There was a pause and then a kindly response: "I understand."

Artie didn't know what else to say. Jeffrey asked, "You're okay, aren't you? You're not upset by what happened?"

"Oh, no," said Artie. "I'm fine. And thanks very much for dinner. It was really good. Well, I guess I should go now. I guess I'll see you around Warble House."

He didn't mention that the possibility he was truly needed was something too thrilling for his self-loathing psyche to acknowledge. It was easier to leave Jeffrey with the impression that he was a little fawn who had been trifled with and probably damaged for life.

Artie had got used to feeling sorry for his put-upon self, but getting off the phone with Jeffrey, he felt pretty much like what Elizabeth would have called a schmuck.

"Aw, jeepers," said Homer Blomberg, looking up from his book and recognizing Artie Dunne. "Well, siddown," he said, indicating the wooden chair across from the outrageously Naugahydebound Barcalounger dominating his office in the Brown English department. Artie walked toward the seat that had been his during innumerable conferences when Homer had been his adviser for his thesis on Keats. Their relationship was based on the affectionate pretense that each couldn't stand wasting his time in the other's presence; they had developed it into a kind of vaudeville routine. Sitting down, Artie noticed the familiar prints of Jane Eyre and Catherine Earnshaw on the wall—Brontë's broads, Homer called them—next to photos of Bette Davis and Katharine Hepburn. Homer Blomberg was the least campy of men: Davis and Hepburn had wall space only because he had never got over the Bijou crushes of his youth, which, like his adulthood, had been spent entirely around Brown and Providence. The only picture that won desk space in the office was a framed one of Homer's beautiful childhood sweetheart and wife, Bessie.

"So what brings you down here?" he asked Artie. "Trying to recapture your misspent youth?"

Like many of Homer's growlings during Artie's undergraduate years, this one hit the psychological nail on the head. "In a way," was all Artie responded. He had come down to Providence on impulse, cutting classes, because he wanted to spend the day in a place he knew he would be fully accepted, sexually inapplicable and required to do nothing. Homer's office was the place.

"Since when are you such a child of few words?" asked Homer, who favored such circumlocutions, S. J. Perelman being the greatest writer to have come out of Providence and, in Homer's estimation, off the planet. "And how come you want it back, in any case? As youth goes, it was, we seem to agree, misspent. Besides, I thought your last 6-cent cardboard missive mentioned something relative to your being about to teach freshmen, a sufficiently adult, if frustrating, occupation—and, of course, one more way in which fair Brunonia exceeds the place you are. We wouldn't dare let somebody as ignorant as yourself loose on the gurgling frosh."

"Yeah, I'm teaching," Artie said. "I made them completely rethink everything they knew about modern poetry the other day."

"Multiplying by zero leaves zero. If you'd come to this university in the days before you were allowed to take thirty-two courses in folk music, and been forced to take some mathematics, you'd know that. Anyway," Homer continued, "how are you finding them? Obstreperous?"

"Actually pretty nice. Except for this one kid named Bukovsky, who talks like Cicero or something."

"Which is to say he had a classical education, no doubt, which you in your yahooism could still profit from. A real pain in the ass, huh? Well, remember how much of a one you could be a mere several seasons ago."

Artie thought Homer might be recalling the day when he had dismissed Homer's statement that *Antony and Cleopatra* was the greatest of Shakespeare's plays by saying Homer liked it because it was "a tragedy about incipient geriatrics."

"So," Homer inquired, "what about the learning side of things?—a side you much more need to be on than the teaching one, by the way. Is it any better than last semester, when it was reported, by however unreliable a source—i.e., yourself—to be, I believe the word is 'lousy'?"

"Nah," said Artie, "it's still lousy. It's all nitpicking. And this constant insistence on what's major and what's minor."

"So what's the problem? You should feel right at home with that. You're the one always talking about what's good and what's bad."

"Yeah," said Artie, "but that's a little less pseudoscientific than this major-minor stuff. Oh, I don't know. Maybe you're right. For once."

"I still say," said Homer, "that you ought to become a journalist—if what you want to do is tell people what they ought to be reading instead of explaining it to them. Besides, your style is sufficiently meretricious to be up to the job."

"Thanks," said Artie, disgustedly. "God, *jour*nalism."

"So what's wrong with being a journalist? What the hell do you think Plato was? He just went around and covered the philosophical waterfront and then hotfooted it back to the papyrus to put down what he'd heard. Now everybody treats him like Aquinas. He was actually more like Winchell. It's a living, too, which is more than you're likely to make once you get out of Ma Harvard's arms. Of course, Uncle Sam may take care of your employment soon. How old are you, anyway? Twenty-two? That's plenty young enough. You may be over in Saudi Arabia next winter, fighting for the vital fluids of my oil burner. By the way, how's that drug addict you used to hang out with?"

"Oh," said Artie. "You mean Shane Manningham. He's in California working for his brother. But I haven't heard from him in a while."

"So, aside from being harassed by child geniuses and academic relativists, you're all alone in the world. I may weep."

"You should know the half of it," Artie said, in his best I'm-going-to-eat-worms voice.

"Aw, no. On your feet. Bessie's cooking spaetzle. Let's go home and have her fill your face. You can bellyache to her."

After taking ample portions of Bessie's noodles and sympathy, and after it was decided he would spend the night on the sofa bed in the room occupied by the Blombergs' parrot, Bruno, Artie excused himself to go to the library, telling his hosts he had a lesson to prepare for tomorrow's comp class. Homer and Bessie said good night, gave him a key to the house and went into the parlor for their evening's reading, which generally ran to Shakespearean comedies and violent detective novels.

Artie left their house on Prospect Street for the Rockefeller Library. The comp class he'd mentioned to them was really just an excuse, because he didn't know how to explain that what he really wanted to do tonight was commune with the aroma of the

B-level stacks. His faith in the therapeutic powers of Mrs. Crangel remained strong, but he wished to try more mystical remedies for his confusion. Maybe if he inhaled the smell of the bindings in the aisles that housed "Keats, John, Works By and About," he would find his emotional chaos spinning itself toward order. He was in pursuit of epiphany, not analysis.

Crossing Waterman Street, he looked up at Carrie Tower, recalling the night Shane had forced him to climb it, with an eye toward throwing water-filled condoms on the pedestrians below. Once inside and up, they had been so thrilled by the assortment of lights and steeples and courtyards and parks beneath them that they became too embarrassed to carry out their mission and instead talked about the meaning of life.

Once in the B-level stacks, Artie went directly to the Keats shelves, shutting his eyes and breathing in the odors he had lived with night after night four years before. He picked out Clarence Thorpe's selection of the poems and letters and opened it to the charge-card pocket in back. The stamp of his identification card was still readable:

A V Dunne '73
ETHELBERT 223
BOX 1475
1969–70

The book had been due on May 10, 1970. Artie remembered how irrelevant that date had seemed even to his rule-abiding soul during the season of the strike.

He brought the book to the carrel where he used to sit, sometimes for whole days and late into the night. Shane would drop by with news of what was happening in the dorms, hung with bed sheets stenciled with fists and vibrating with the odd, ugly joy of those days. Now, in 1974, as a different generation of undergraduates studied around him, Artie could almost feel Shane standing over him and saying, "This ode stuff must be really potent, Urn Man. You don't know what you're missing upstairs. Some eighty-year-old philosopher emeritus was just screaming 'Fuck the Army!' into the microphone while this black chick in boots up to her behind French-kissed him her congrats. Why don't you take a break and check it out? Or do you just want me to bring you another goddamned apple?"

That was, in fact, all that Artie, on fire with a love of words for the first time, could ask for. Just another apple and another visit from Shane—and, in between, those poems.

As he sat here four years later, it was hard for him not to wish that Shane would suddenly materialize to take him out of his present quandaries. But something adult in him knew what an idle desire this was. Could Shane really tell him what to do with Jeffrey's needs, Angela's extravagances? No more than he could study umlaut and pass the M.A. exams for him. Staring at the old charge card, Artie realized that even on May 10, 1970, his present had been sneaking up from behind, waiting for its appointment with him: Angela had been in her flat in Knightsbridge; Jeffrey had been in New Haven; even the demons had been somewhere in his own central nervous system, waiting for the signals that would dispatch them to his outermost ganglia. And just as certainly, whatever would be in his life four years from now was already stealing a march on him. Who else could live that life but himself?

This was not the epiphany he had been hoping for, but it was an insight nonetheless.

> *How then are Souls to be made? How then are these sparks which are God to have identity given them—so as ever to possess a bliss peculiar to each one's individual existence? How but by the medium of a world like this? . . . Do you not see how necessary a World of Pains and troubles is to school an Intelligence and make it a Soul? A Place where the heart must feel and suffer in a thousand diverse ways.*

He had first read these words — just JK dashing off a few random thoughts to the folks — in the very volume before him. But had he ever really taken them to heart?

Maybe it was the word "Pains," or maybe it was "Intelligence" that made Artie think he should right now try to deal with the particular portion of his here-and-now that was Angela. He hadn't spoken to her since the morning-after at Jeffrey's, and that was two days ago. Resolute, he got up, ran two dollar bills through the change machine and went to a pay phone in the reading room.

She wasn't home. So he called Elizabeth's.

"Oh, it's you," she said with relief. "I thought it might be Little Nell. She's called twice tonight for advice about this paper she's writing for Blankman. It's on methods of mutilation in Poe — with, I gather, a few tasty digressions to harpoon motifs in *Moby-Dick*. I'm telling ya, Downing didn't know what she was doing to that girl when she sent her Juan Perón or whoever it was. Nah, she's not here. But she was around dinnertime. We watched *Candlepins for Cash* over pizza and champagne. She just got word she's won some prize for the best graduate essay on an Elizabethan subject — you know, one of those things endowed in memory of Radcliffe chicks with names like Sarah Jane Titmouse who kicked off around 1905? Angela batted out a few thousand words on *Coriolanus* one night last month in England — when she was bored, she says — and so naturally she's just cleaned up. She came in here tonight with a new pair of shoes which must've gone for slightly more than my net worth. Hang on, I gotta conk a roach with my fuzzy."

Artie heard the receiver clatter to a kitchen counter and then the sound of one of Elizabeth's slippers beating the daylights out of a household insect. "Gotcha, motherfucker," she said in the distance before returning to the line.

"I'm back," she said. "So anyway, that's the last I've seen of her. I tell ya, she's a witch, ya know? I mean, she's uncanny.

We're watching the tube, and every time somebody gets up to bowl, she'll look at the ball go down the alley and say, 'He'll get four pins,' and I swear, every time but one she guessed right. The one time she missed she said, 'Bad camera work.' Maybe it was a rerun? Anyway, I don't know where she gets the time to be bored. I'm in a total panic, working my butt off with the reading list. You too? If you want something else to worry about, by the way, Richard hasn't done douche-worth since October. I think he still thinks he's got my century, too. We're gonna fuck up that exam something awful, I just know it, and get tossed out on our tushies, all except her."

"So you think we should just go on like before?" Artie asked Angela.

"Why ever not?" she responded.

They were lying on the forty-nine-square-foot bed looking at the television, which Angela was turning into a sort of strobe cube by continually pressing the channel buttons on her remote control. They were watching, more or less simultaneously, the *Tonight* show, *Mrs. Miniver* ("silly cow") and *The Man from U.N.C.L.E.* ("Good idea getting that Celt to play the Russki. The real Ivans are *so* plain.")

Tomorrow, he thought, he would work for eighteen hours after teaching his class. He would begin to get his reading under control. But what about everything else? Was it really all right for him to be here with Angela? When he didn't think she loved him? During Christmas vacation he had been ready to demand an answer to the question of whether or not she did. Now, after what had happened with Jeffrey, he wasn't in a position to demand anything. Could she really think it was all right herself? He tried to ferret out some clues as she kept annihilating each picture on the screen in favor of the next.

"Angela, remember that note you passed me during the Symposium, way back in October? The one with the couplet?"

"Vaguely, darling," she said, making the screen change an image of Ed McMahon selling Alpo to one of Greer Garson kissing Walter Pidgeon.

"Well, you said there were two that you'd like to . . . you know . . ."

"Screw," said Angela.

"That's the word," said Artie, who had learned from Mrs. Crangel to mock his own primness. "Well, who was the other?"

"Why, Richard, I suppose," she answered. "After all, he's perfectly presentable, if not quite running on nuclear energy."

Presentable, Artie thought. Was that the only test?

"How about the other part? Remember? You said there were three you'd like to kill. I assume Canker and Branded were two of them. Who was the third?"

"Oh, love, I don't remember," Angela yawned, deeply bored and flipping over to *The Man from U.N.C.L.E.* "One wants to kill so *many* people, doesn't one?"

13

In the weeks before spring vacation, Artie continued with Angela much as before. He showed up for sessions with Mrs. Crangel and saw the demons recede again into manageableness. He attended and taught classes, watched Patricia Hearst become the creature of her captors and saw the ring tighten around Richard Nixon. But more than anything else he worked, reading late into each night, even while at Angela's, racing through text after text in an effort to prepare himself for the May exams. The special-edition American literature summary he was making for her, as well as the more compact one for Elizabeth and Richard, continued to fatten and to make greater historical sense. But in everything else he was behind: Spenser blended into Sidney; Samuel Daniel entangled Wyatt; it was impossible to keep one Warton separate from another or to remember that Ford Madox Ford's grandfather was Ford Madox Brown.

There were now also freshman essays to mark. In quality these ranged from Adam Bukovsky's grandiloquence to near illiteracy. Those in the lowest part of the range — Harvard students! — made Artie realize that compared to what was going on in some parts of the country, his own inadequate public schooling had been on the order of what John Stuart Mill's father dished out to his kid.

Angela organized a number of sessions at her apartment during which the two of them, along with Elizabeth and Richard, were supposed to discuss the books they were reading for the exams. But these occasions proved more social than studious, excuses for Angela to pass around the vodka bottle and get them to stay for Chinese take-out and *The Streets of San Francisco.*

The last Symposium before spring vacation was so severely ossified that it was hard to believe the class could keep meeting for another whole month before the M.A. exams. Canker and Branded were back to the selves they had displayed for most of the fall, their Angela-arranged liaisons apparently having proved less durable than Little Nell's. Even Nell seemed bored with the class these days, literary raptures being, it would seem, dull weather compared to those enforced by Rodrigo. Artie at one point heard her absently humming "The Way We Were," which was playing everywhere that year, as Canker and Branded conducted their mutual admiration and tut-tutting. The text today was Oscar Wilde's "The Decay of Lying," and the two of them were shaking their heads over its queer non-neoclassical notion that life should imitate art, not vice versa. "A perversity," said Canker. "Mere cleverness," echoed Branded. Richard was asleep. Elizabeth, true to a vow to regard the class as a weekly holiday, continued with *I Promessi Sposi.* Artie was using the two hours as study time, careering through an anthology of Puritan American essays. He had learned to screen out the academic Muzak produced by Canker and Branded, but about an hour into class an unfamiliar sound broke through to his attention.

It was the sound of crying: soft, muffled sniffles into a tissue. It was getting more audible and anguished, too. Artie looked around to see where it was coming from and then his eyes settled on the source—Angela.

Crying?

Oh my God, maybe she's finally cracking up over what I did with Jeffrey, maybe we're going to have a baby, maybe there really is someone else and she's afraid the news will destroy me. She's going to blurt it out in front of the class. She does have feelings.

Within a minute or two Angela's distress was loud enough so that even Branded and Canker had to pay attention. The latter, exhibiting the unease he always displayed when forced to regard the messy things others deemed real life, croaked, "Miss Downing?"

"Oh," said Angela, looking up with a startled expression. "I'm terribly sorry. I had no idea I was making such a nuisance of myself. I apologize. Please carry on."

But her crying continued, increasing in intensity and finally going over the lachrymal border between sniffles and sobs.

"Miss Downing?" an excruciated Canker felt compelled to repeat. "Are you certain you're all right?"

"Oh, yes," said Angela, crying harder than ever. "Well, really, no," she said, new tears pouring out.

"Well, what is the trouble?" asked Canker, actually scratching himself in discomfort.

"Sir," said Angela, wiping her eyes and appearing to try to regain composure, "it's the text. It's what you've been saying about 'The Decay of Lying.' Frankly, up until this moment I've held my tongue because I was hesitant to inject any commentary that might be so subjective as to be useless. But I'm afraid I must speak. The comments made by yourself and Mr. Branded deeply wound me. You have been trivializing something very dear to my heart"—renewed sobs—"and to my family." (Quizzical expressions throughout the room; a look of infinite puzzlement from Artie.) "You see, shortly after Oscar Wilde left the prison to which he was confined for nothing more than his own particular expressions of affection"—here she shot a glance toward Artie; he threw his gaze down to the writings of Increase Mather—"he went, as we all know, to France. What most of us don't know, however, is that sometime after his arrival there he met a beautiful woman of great charity with whom he fell deeply in love. In a letter to her which has never been published—indeed, which is in my possession—Oscar Wilde told her that of all his writings he had always considered 'The Decay of Lying' the most"—long pause—"seminal. He wrote her that he still wished to believe its words, but that it had now become difficult for him to put faith in them, because in her, so much a part of *life*, he had found a beauty to which no art could ever aspire." (Little Nell's eyes crinkled empathetically.) "But she wrote back and told him that he must never change his ideas, because much as the charm of her life had quickened his, it was reading his thoughts about art which had sent her imagination soaring to heights it would otherwise never have seen. Sir"—by now Angela was speaking through great facial contortions and unstoppable cataracts—"that letter reached Oscar Wilde on the day he died." She waved her hand to indicate she was all right and they mustn't assist her. She composed herself and spoke low and slowly. "Shortly before his death, he and the woman conceived a child. That baby, sir"—and here Angela's sobs resumed—"was my grandmother."

"Are you *crazy?* Are you *nuts?* Are you out of your goddamned *mind?*" Artie, reaching unusual levels of volume and profanity, shouted at Angela that night in her apartment. "Not one *word* of that was true! Do you think they *believe* you? What were you trying to *prove?*"

"I was bored," Angela said, yawning and flipping through a profile of Chad Everett in an old *TV Guide*. "Aren't you ever bored?"

"Of course I am. Sometimes." In fact, he knew, rarely. He was much more likely to be ecstatic, terrified, jumpy or confused. It was true that he wasn't beyond being bored by things like the Symposium, but on the whole boredom was something of which he had scant awareness.

"Well?" Angela asked, wearily.

"Don't you care that once they realize, 'Hey, this isn't true,' they're going to think, 'Boy, has this girl got problems'? Don't you care about what they're going to think?"

"Darling, in this world there does not exist the electron microscope capable of discovering the dimensions of my worry over their opinion of me."

"Well, I care what they think."

"I never doubted that for a moment. Tell me, if they give you a little gold star, will that make you feel like a real person?"

"You know, Angela, if you're accusing me of being childish, you ought to look at all these stupid little pranks you pull, like some *ennui*-ridden Marie Antoinette. You call them adult? Do *they* make *you* feel like a real person?"

"Tell me something else. Just what sort of person, real or unreal, do you think I am?"

"I've got no idea."

"Well, why don't you make some fucking effort to find out!" she shouted. "And I don't mean asking me a lot of questions in a pathetic little New Year's letter and expecting me to send you back some answers you can memorize as if they came from a Barnes and Noble outline. I mean doing a little work!"

She went into the bedroom. Artie stared at the door she had slammed between them, surprised by her anger. It was real anger, something he'd never seen her exhibit before. And he had provoked it. He *was* a real person. Maybe not to Harvard, but to her.

He did not go home to Long Island for spring vacation. He remained in Comus, working on the M.A. reading list, especially the American literature summaries he had to render to Angela and the group in just a few weeks. He spent whole days at his desk, reading through Robert Frost and Amy Lowell and Ezra Pound and a dozen other writers, dappling the books beside his plate with the crumbs of makeshift meals.

Comus seemed more or less quiet. But on Thursday evening of the vacation Artie could hear sobs coming from Voltears's room across the hall. This in itself was not unusual, but by attending to the noise, Artie could detect two sets of tear ducts, instead of one, at work. There was apparently commiseration, not just lonely anguish, going on. He got up from his reading of Amy Lowell—whose hefty oglings of John Keats he would never forgive—and investigated.

The other set of ducts belonged to Willard Gill, who was repeating again and again to Voltears, "I don't know how this could have happened."

What had happened, it turned out, was that Willard had finished his dissertation. "Suddenly," he told a gathering crowd on the third floor, "my adviser of twenty-three years says to me this afternoon, 'Willard, it's over. You've got two hundred and eighty pages, some of them dating back to the Truman administration. You've done enough. This fish is caught. Reel it in. Skin it. It's over. Stop right where you are. Not another chapter. You'll get your degree. I'll sign the papers.' "

Willard was still in shock. He had, everyone knew, really expected to go on writing and rewriting and procrastinating and starting over for at least several more years. Now he would have to go out and find a job. From the sarcasm of his ichthyological metaphors, Artie supposed that the professor could, after more than a fifth of a century, bear no more of Willard's fits and starts.

"You poor thing," the Gainsborough boy said, massaging Willard's middle-aged shoulders.

"Tough break, Willard," said the Pithecanthropus, who was paying a rare weeknight visit.

"Here, drink this," said the Mad Doorknob Polisher, handing Willard a cup of tea.

"Is sad, you know?" said the Spanish philosophy student to the Chinese physics student.

Artie was beginning to get the hang of grading papers. Spotting such infelicities as "She probed herself" (the description of a heroine's introspection), he would now write comments like "God, I hope not" in the margin. The humanities majors largely ignored these. The pre-meds applied them with tremendous zeal whenever there were rewrites required. One future neurologist used the phrase "In today's modern world"; Artie put a line between "today's" and "modern" and wrote "redundant" under it. When the essay was resubmitted, the phrase was revised to read, "In today's redundant modern world."

More and more he enjoyed being "on the other side of the desk," as graduate students invariably put it. He liked acting like a lock-master on a river, opening and shutting sluices for the students' liveliness to pour through. Sometimes, though, classes took on a life of their own, and any restraints imposed by him would be useless. On April 2 they were doing D. H. Lawrence's *The Virgin and the Gypsy*. Near the end of the hour a girl who often made feminist observations pronounced Yvette's hunger for the Charles Bronson–like gypsy to be "grotesque."

"Aw, he's good for the bitch," replied a boy across the room.

"Right, Ray, and when we get to the New Amazonia, your balls are going on the first Christmas tree."

Artie was left with an appalled expression on his face when the bell rang. "Don't worry about them, Mr. Dunne," said a sympathetic boy from Texas as he left the room. "They must justa gotten up on the wrong side of the bed. They've been goin' out together for months."

Oh, no, Artie thought. *It's his brother.*

"Hello, is Shane there?"

The voice on the other end came back curt and angry. "No, he is not."

"Do you know when he'll be back?" Artie continued, though eager to be off the line.

"No, I do not. In fact, I can pretty much assure you that he won't *be* back. He hasn't been here for two weeks, and is therefore, in my patient estimation, unemployed."

"Did he leave a forwarding address?" Artie asked.

"He left nothing except for one pair of filthy gym shorts and a sort of bobby pin that I gather is used in the administration of small remnants of illegal narcotics to oneself. Have you got any more questions?" the voice snapped.

"No, sir," said Artie.

"Good," said Bill Manningham, slamming down the phone in Silicon Valley.

What about June twenty-eighth? Artie thought.

"Hi, Artie," said Jeffrey Stanhope as he walked up the steps of Warble House.

"Oh, hi," said Artie, as he walked, more quickly, down them.

"All I can think about are these exams!" Artie said, explaining to Mrs. Crangel why he couldn't keep his mind on any of her questions.

"Not even about Angela?"

"No," said Artie, "not even about Angela. Anyway, she's mad at me."

"Why?"

"Because she says she's bored. And that I'm not helping because all I do is study. But what else can I do? Anyway, she's not just bored in a regular way. She's superbored. She barely leaves her apartment anymore. She cuts most of her classes. She watches television and she shops. And she'll still ace the exams."

"Do you resent that?" Mrs. Crangel asked.

"Resent what?" Artie asked back, perplexed. "Her having things come so easily to her?"

"Her being bored with you."

"She's bored with *school.*"

"Oh," said Mrs. Crangel. "In any case, I thought you weren't thinking about her. I thought all you could think about were the exams."

"That's right," said Artie, agitated. "Those exams mean *every-*

thing. If I don't pass each one of them, I can't go on and do my Ph.D. If I do badly on them, I'll have a terrible reputation in the department for the whole rest of the time I'm in graduate school. I can't think about *anything else* right now. Not Angela, not Shane, *nothing*."

"You probably don't even have time to put your hands in your pockets." She smiled.

"That's right," said Artie, brimming with energy. "I've *got* to do well on these tests. I've got to shut everything else out 'til they're over. They're my whole future. If I don't do well on them, nothing else will go right while I'm here. And if I don't finish my degree, I'll never get to teach."

"And you've decided you want to teach?" Mrs. Crangel asked.

"Yes," said Artie, still bouncing like a fighter before a match, "I do."

"Then you've answered one big question, no?" said Mrs. Crangel.

Artie, not catching her use of the lingo of their first session, way back in October, simply said, "I've got to do well on those goddamned tests."

"Well, shee-it," Mrs. Crangel said.

"Will you stop *reading!*" Angela screamed, racing across the living room, ripping a volume of Emily Dickinson's poems out of Artie's hand and hitting him, hard, on the head with it.

"Ouch," he said, without much alarm, being by now used to this sort of thing from her. He picked up the volume of Walt Whitman that was the next on his pile and opened it instead.

Once more Angela tore the book from his hands. "Oh, how charming. Walt Whitman, the good gay poet. 'On Cruising Brooklyn Fairy.' Did you and Stanhope read all this aloud to one another in bed?"

"Thanks," said Artie, getting up and walking toward the door. "Thanks a lot."

Angela went and fetched him by the shoulders. "Oh, love," she whispered contritely. "Please forgive. It's just that I'm so spitlessly, shatteringly bored. I thought if I can't get you to do anything else, maybe I can at least get you to fight."

"Okay. I'm sorry, too," said Artie, turning around and going limp in her arms, as in what they were already beginning to think of as "the old days" of late fall. "It's just that I've *got* to do well on these exams."

Angela, seizing the moment, said, "I know. But why don't we just engage in a teeny-weeny bit of lovemaking right now? Afterward you can go straight back to the hermitess and the homo."

They went into the bedroom and made love as they often did, without shutting off the television. Artie always found this slightly bizarre, but it didn't bother Angela until they heard the late news program that evening—"This afternoon in California the parents of Patricia Hearst, alias Tania . . ."—which showed the inevitable photograph of Patty and her gun in front of the SLA banner.

Angela growled, "I am so thoroughly sick of that Bolshevik tart," and hit the remote control button with Artie's elbow, which until a moment before had been more or less in her mouth.

"Oh, good," she said. "Some substance at last." Johnny Carson was talking to Fernando Lamas about Esther Williams. Angela resumed kissing Artie's elbow as he stroked her breasts and tried to remember whether it was more accurate to classify Emily Dickinson as a Transcendental Calvinist or a Calvinistic Transcendentalist.

Ten days before the M.A. exams Angela's group met in her apartment to exchange their summaries.

Richard's was very short, and he apologized. "I'd tell you I did my best, but lying is too hard. I just hope you don't feel too ripped off."

"Not in the least, darling," said Angela. In truth, Artie and

Elizabeth did feel a little ripped off, but they liked Richard too much to fuss, and had, in any case, expected this.

Elizabeth's summary of the nineteenth-century list was intelligent and succinct. Artie, who had had to race through some of the novels on that list so quickly that the plots were mixed up in his head (he had all the wrong people married to each other in *Middlemarch*), was energetically grateful. "This is terrific, Elizabeth," he said, avidly flipping through his copy. "Just terrific."

"Thanks, squirt," she replied. The two of them had become buddies in the course of the year. Baffled by Richard's laziness and Angela's nerve, they continued to share the Ellis Island mentality about Harvard. They didn't quite know how they had washed up on these shores, or if it was the right idea, but now that they were here, they were going to make good.

Angela's summary was a work of art. She had dictated it in the course of two evenings to a professional stenographer she had hired for $10 an hour. The typing, done for another $8 an hour, was flawless. The summary wasn't even Xeroxed. She had had it offset and then put into four leather binders with the names Elizabeth Bergbaum, Richard Marbury, Arthur Dunne and Angela Downing embossed in gold letters on the different covers. The luggage shop that did the embossing had delivered the copies two hours ago. Angela's hands hadn't touched paper, ink or typewriter.

"Jesus, Angela," said Elizabeth, "this is the closest I'll get to Gucci in my lifetime."

Artie's summary of American literature was like the genre itself—voluminous, breathless, occasionally very good, highly disorganized and very eager to please. He was still fiddling with paper clips and manila folders as the other three extended their hands to receive copies. "Well," said Angela, who still thought Calvin Coolidge was a novelist, "here it is. Huckleberry Finn's first year at Harvard." She took her special, expanded edition and put it on her coffee table next to copies of the poems of Robert

Herrick and Harold Robbins's *Seventy-Nine Park Avenue*—the only work of American literature visible in her apartment.

For the next ten days, at every moment he wasn't sitting in a class or teaching one, or making small concessions to Angela, Artie studied the summaries. Somewhere in them lay the secrets of the tests. But what exactly would come up? What configurations would they be asked to make of these centuries of plays, rhymes, arguments, fictions, polemics, some of them older than the troubadours, a handful newer than the atom bomb? Even Angela couldn't predict the questions for sure. He reread, memorized, related and speculated himself into a dizzy haze of genres and centuries.

Some of the late-April evenings managed to defy the constant likelihood of raw spring rain in Cambridge, and when it was warm, Artie opened his window and cracked his door, something he'd not done since October. One night, poring over Angela's remarks on revenge tragedy, he felt a hand on his shoulder. He jumped. "Sorry, honey," said the Gainsborough boy. "I just thought maybe you could use this." He handed Artie a cup of tea. "William just made a fresh pot."

"Oh," said Artie. "Thanks. Who's William?"

The Gainsborough boy looked at him a little incredulously. "You know. *William*. Down the hall?"

Artie realized he meant the Mad Doorknob Polisher and that he had lived in Comus for eight months without knowing his real name.

"Oh," he said, faintly ashamed to be drinking the guy's tea after he'd reduced him to some capitalized character out of Lewis Carroll. But the last thing he had time for now was learning yet one more name. *In fact, was it Warton or Warburton who . . .* Sipping the tea, he tried to check this point in Richard's flimsy write-up of the eighteenth century.

He knew it was mad, but it was the only way he could get Angela to let him study in peace for the final few days before the exams: he agreed they would spend the night before the tests on the town in Boston. "Oh, darling, you can drink club soda, and I'll see you're tucked in by midnight. We'll even pretend you have a big football game in the morning, and won't make even one tiny roll on the big bass drum before we say nighty-night."

So on the first evening in May, Artie, red-eyed and fact-filled, found himself sitting with Angela, Richard and Elizabeth in a lounge of the Copley Plaza Hotel. A tired, balding pianist, who seemed to be a substitute, was creating an uncertain ambience by interweaving Gershwin songs with numbers like "My Favorite Things." "Oh, puke," said Elizabeth. "Play something bearable."

As it was, she was only attending with one ear. The other held the ear plug of a transistor radio over which she was catching the late innings of a Red Sox game. "It calms me down," she said when Angela rolled her eyes in dismay. "Quiet," she said, listening hard. "Here comes Yaz."

During this exchange Richard was at another table, talking to an old Amherst-days girlfriend he'd bumped into. Artie, taking advantage of the conversation Elizabeth and Angela entered into after Yaz walked, stealthily withdrew from his pocket a few folded pages of his nineteenth-century summary and rested them on the banquette, where he thought Angela wouldn't be able to spot them. All he wanted to do was make sure he had a few more distinctions between Coleridge and Dr. Johnson down pat.

The pianist had swung into "A Summer Place" when he felt a cold rush of liquid in his crotch. He started, bumping Angela's head as she poured the last ice cubes from a glass of vodka into his pants.

She smiled lethally. "I do *so* hate people who break their promises, don't you?"

"I'm sorry," said Artie, embarrassed not only by his double dealing but by what the men's room attendant was going to think.

In order to make it up to Angela, he assented to spending one hour at Satan, halfway across town. "Yeah," agreed Elizabeth to this new plan, "let's go. I can't take any more of this dork at the keyboard." Within a half hour—Angela having paid a short BU sophomore they found on Boylston Street $25 for his dry pants—they were all on the dance floor.

Running on seltzer and adrenaline and hardly any sleep, Artie flailed away, no more competently than he had in the fall, to the strains of "Rock the Boat." Lightheaded from all the work and tension, he soon drifted into unexpected euphoria, watching Angela's beautiful hair and body wave through the infernal glamour of the strobe lights. Dreamily aroused now, enough to think it might be all right to break training when they got back to her apartment, he danced toward her and, violating all the rules of disco, took her in his arms and sort of foxtrotted for a while.

She smiled down at him and kissed his hair. Into his ear she whispered, "It did have its moments, didn't it, love?"

14

One measure of Artie's lack of romantic experience was the fact that it wasn't until several minutes past midnight, by which time he was out of the BU sophomore's pants and tucked into bed, alone, in Comus, that he realized he'd been dumped. When Angela made her remark about its having had "its moments," he hadn't understood what she meant, but now the tense and import of her observation were unmistakable. She was getting rid of him, the way she might trade in a car with two hundred miles on it or give a twice-worn sweater to the Goodwill: on some whim of disgust.

When they'd finished dancing, he could now recall, something unusual had happened. She had been reasonable. She'd said something like, "I suppose we all ought to get home," and a few minutes later was driving the four of them back to Cambridge. The first stop she made was Comus, which Artie had at the time—ten minutes ago—attributed to further reasonableness; she'd decided he really ought to go straight to bed, not even stay up talking, much less making love, at her apartment.

But why had she stopped at Comus *first*, when by all rights the easiest thing to do was drop Elizabeth off on Putnam Avenue? Just Angela's typically directionless driving? No, he now thought, there was method to her meandering. She wanted to get rid of him while Richard and Elizabeth were still in the car, wanted to avoid his questions, avoid the need to do some definitive dumping *à deux*. Too messy. Too *tedious*, he fumed, eyes wide open in the dark.

This couldn't be happening, not the night before the tests. Then again, why shouldn't it? What probability had any of the year had? This wasn't improbable; it was fitting. It rounded things off with a nice symmetry. She'd let him out of the car in the same spot where Shane had said bye-bye at the beginning of the fall. Why didn't they just dump him out, gangland style, and let his body roll to the door?

Symmetry, inevitability: good words to apply to the later novels of Henry James. Would they come up on part five tomorrow? What were Robert Burton's dates? How did *Our Mutual Friend* end? What would they ask about the pre-Romantics?

He couldn't sleep.

Why had she done it? Just because he'd brought notes to the Copley Plaza?

Which was more significant to the development of English drama? *Gammer Gurton's Needle* or *Ralph Roister Doister*?

Had its fucking *moments*.

Two o'clock. He was doomed.

How could he pass the tests?

How had he failed her?

After perhaps two hours' sleep, during which he appeared trouserless and unrehearsed in a series of dreams, Artie heard his alarm go off. He sprang toward the bathroom down the hall. Comus was collectively rising. From behind Willard's door he detected sounds of packing and muttering: "It's not fair. It's just not fair." From the showers he could hear the Gainsborough boy doing half a rendition of "Something Wonderful," his upper registers counterpointed by the Pithecanthropus's basso profundo.

It was a reasonably tranquil morning, so as Artie got back to his room and dressed, he thought it would be quiet enough for him to do some last-minute cramming. He sat down at his desk and took out his summaries.

And then he froze. There was just too much to know and understand. There had been too many poets, too many centuries, too many genres into which words had been poured and arranged. Panic swept him, and his hands went into the pockets of the BU sophomore's pants.

He thought of calling Mrs. Crangel. But she didn't get to her office until ten. He thought of calling Shane. But he didn't know where he was. He thought of calling Angela. But she probably wouldn't even hear the phone for the sounds of her hair dryer and *Captain Kangaroo.*

And, besides, she had dumped him.

He would have to do it on his own. He opened up the first summary, of medieval literature, and made himself concentrate. The first title his eyes fell on was *Le Morte d'Arthur*, by Malory. This wasn't auspicious, but he kept flipping through the pages, stopping to read a few entries, convincing himself he could still remember and think.

By 8:30 he had recovered enough confidence to try imagining what some of the big questions might be. He gathered up his pens and left the room, wondering: *Let's say they ask us to outline the essential differences between the first generation of English romantic poets (Blake, Wordsworth, Coleridge) and the second (Byron, Shelley and—last but not least—Keats). What would I say?*

Now, if he knew any of the material at all, he knew this part of it. But how would he organize his essay? What would he begin by saying? He'd have to think fast and coherently. Would he be able to do it? Would nonsense come out? Or nothing at all? In another moment of panic he realized he simply couldn't think of how he would start to answer that question. His mind seemed not blank but too full. Out in the hall he froze. If he couldn't, *this minute*, think of the first sentence of an answer, he knew that he would enter Cleaver under a cloud of fear and hopelessness. He had to think of something *now* if he was to have any chance at all.

Nothing would come. There seemed no way to clarify his brain.

Then something occurred to him.

He looked around. The hall seemed empty. Willard must have left. The Gainsborough boy and the Pithecanthropus must have gone to breakfast. He had the hall to himself. It was worth a try.

Walking backward a few steps, he readied himself, crouched into position and sprang, running to the wall at the end of the hall and flinging himself against its brown bricks.

"Ouch!" he shouted, and the next sentence that formed in his mind began: "Whereas the first generation of English romantic poets began their careers partly in the shadow of the great neo-classicists . . ."

There was a story about oral exams (which would be taken in two years by those successful on today's M.A. tests), purportedly true, known to every graduate student in the English department. It concerned the Ph.D. candidate who was so nervous in front of his examiners that he kept his ankles rigidly crossed (in order to keep his knees from knocking) and his fists furiously clenched for the entire two-and-one-half-hour grilling. When it was over and he was invited to stand up, he did so, not realizing that his legs had fallen asleep. He fell over. Attempting to minimize injury and embarrassment, he tried to break his fall with his outstretched arms. But his nails had dug so tightly into his palms for the two and a half hours that his hands were bleeding. He succeeded in breaking the fall, but not without leaving two bloody palm prints on the carpet.

Artie was thinking about this story as he sat in Cleaver Hall —the same room where Greek met in the mornings—and waited with the twenty other students for the blue books to be brought in. Though relieved that his go at wall banging had unclogged his mind, he was nonetheless amazed by the poise of those around him. Elizabeth was calmly reading through the last chapters of

I Promessi Sposi; Richard was dozing; Little Nell was braiding strips of leather into what Artie hoped was a key chain.

Angela was reading *Vogue*. She didn't look at him.

Joseph Branded walked in at the elbow of Wallace Canker, who was carrying the question sheets and blue books. At the sight of these papers, Artie's heart switched into what Shane used to call "hummingbird overdrive." Panic-stricken once again, he turned to look at Angela. She was reassuring the person next to her by opening her mouth in a huge, theatrical yawn.

"As you all know," said Wallace Canker, poised to distribute the exams, "the results of your performance on the examinations will be announced in approximately two weeks' time. Shortly thereafter I look forward to seeing you all at some festivities in Chauncey House, at which time we can all regard our achievements of the past year with nostalgia and satisfaction."

"Oh, puke," Artie heard Elizabeth whisper.

Then the test got under way. After one more surge of fright, he set to work. Within two hours it was apparent that the lifelong skills that had made him—again, Shane's words—"such a goddamned, grindy little wonk" had not deserted him. Once rolling, he cut through the "ID's" and organized his essays with the aplomb of a born test taker, a lifer in the groves of academe. He knew what he was doing. He saw English literature, and he saw it in pieces, just as the exams wanted him to. He took his hour lunch break alone and in silence. When he returned to Cleaver for the remaining sections, he was confident enough to emit a small groan of derision over a hoary question on the Ancients vs. Moderns controversy that had clearly been composed by Wallace Canker, and even more clearly designed to elicit responses in accord with the works of Wallace Canker. Disregarding Homer Blomberg's old injunction to "butter your own parsnips, not mine" when it came to interpreting things, Artie shamelessly, like a loyal black field hand in *Gone With the Wind*, gave Canker the answers he wanted. Branded himself could not be doing better, he thought as he filled page after page of his third blue book.

More than an hour before time was called, Richard became the first of the twenty to leave, his early departure as much the product of fatigue, Artie knew, as lack of preparation. He had been up for perhaps seven hours straight. Angela stayed in the room, writing steadily and copiously, until there was only a quarter of an hour remaining. This was actually a bit longer than Artie had figured her for. He and Elizabeth were the last to depart, having made use of every available minute to revise and proofread their answers.

On the steps of Cleaver, Artie fell into Elizabeth's arms.

"We did it!" he cried.

"You bet your sweet ass we did," she replied. "C'mon, let's go to Cardell's."

On the serving line Elizabeth heaped her plate with hot open sandwiches and gravy, mashed potatoes, peas, custard, and apple pie. Artie ordered a Coke and Jell-O. Once they sat down, he launched into the sort of manic monologue he would in times past have poured into Shane's sleeve. ". . . And at first I thought, boy, I'll never be able to do this, and I kind of froze when they put the blue books down in front of me and I looked at the stencil and thought, oh boy, how am I ever going to manage, but then I just opened it and, you know, thought, hey, I've got to plunge in, and then I read the first question about medieval verse romances and I suddenly realized, wow, I think I can manage this, and I started writing"—Elizabeth nodded between forkfuls—"and then I thought, well, this stuff on Restoration drama looks a little tricky, but it's really not too bad, and so . . ."

He went on like this for some time, until Elizabeth interrupted him in mid-jabber. "Jesus, look who's here." Angela was coming toward them, carrying a tea-to-go.

"Christ, Downing, what are you doing in this dump? Did the tests unhinge you?"

"The tests?" Angela replied. "Like taking cake from a baby. A very stupid baby. I've got to run, love. Ring me tonight and we'll have a postmortem." She flipped her hair and waved good-bye. She didn't look at Artie, just pointed to his Jell-O and said, "Don't eat that. Really, it's for people in hospital."

When she was gone, Artie, deflated of postexam excitement, turned to Elizabeth. "She's dumped me. What can I do?"

"Get over it," she said, cutting off another piece of hot turkey sandwich.

"That's all?"

"That's plenty."

The normal pressures of the end of the semester, including course exams and essays, actually followed the M.A. tests, but for the next two weeks Artie found his labors more anticlimactic than onerous. He wrote his last essays and managed to differentiate ablaut sufficiently from umlaut to pass the test in the history and structure of the English language.

He heard nothing from Angela and made no efforts to get in touch with her, just cowardly ones at prying information out of Elizabeth, who was reluctant to interfere. He learned that Angela had been spending time in New York, shopping and going to musicals and sloughing off the grime of her year in Warble House.

"Is she with anybody?" Artie asked Elizabeth.

"Hey, squirt, you know better than that. Consult primary sources."

Artie took his last exam on May 20. The next morning—the day of the party for the first-year graduate students—his grades on the M.A. tests arrived. A "1" meant one had scored in the highest quintile. A "5" meant one had landed in the lowest.

A. V. DUNNE	
Medieval	1

Renaissance	1
Restoration to 1800	1
19th and 20th Cents.	2
American	1

This was a miracle, and before he could comprehend or Hail-Mary it, the phone rang.

"Okay," said Elizabeth. "We're friends here. What's the scoop? Whaja get?"

"One, one, one, two, one," said Artie.

"Jesus," she said after whistling reverently.

"I haven't taken it in yet," he responded. "How about you?"

"Two, three, one, two, two. Ever so slightly above average. An intelligent, tasteful, nonshowy showing. But, Jesus, *you*. I can't bear not to tell you, even though it's not my place: you tied Downing. She called a minute ago and told me she got a one, one, one, one, two. A last-minute surge of *ennui* tripped her up on the American, she says. Listen, kid. I audited math several years ago, and I remember this quintile stuff. There's an overwhelming probability you and she are tied for top cheese."

"How about Richard?" was all Artie, his head spinning, could think of to ask. "Do you know?"

"Nah," Elizabeth answered. "But it can't be too good. Anyway, he won't have gotten up to open his mail yet. Speaking of bed, that's where I'm going now. All this relief makes me feel like I haven't slept in a year. My tush is scraping the linoleum. See ya tonight."

Artie sat down and pondered his sudden new status.

He'd gone out a grind and come back a star. How? *It could only be because she dumped me that night*, Artie thought. Surely that was what had given him a prideful surge of mental energy when he walked in and saw her reading *Vogue*. And how had she messed up even a tiny bit? *It could only be because she dumped me that night*. To suffer her fall from perfection on the American literature section? Surely wistful thoughts of him, her guide through that frontier, had been the distraction. 1, 1, 1, 2, 1; 1, 1, 1, 1, 2. Add them up and you got 6 and 6. Box cars. Twelve. Eggs. Apostles. The very hours on the clock. Maybe the two of them weren't preposterous together. Maybe they were a perfect match. Maybe he hadn't known it because he hadn't known *her*. Oh, why hadn't he made "some fucking effort to find out"? Why wasn't she here, thrilling him with her wrath?

Absence from the party would have been impolitic, so even those anguished by 4s and 5s showed up with stiff smiles, wondering if it wasn't deliberate sadism by Canker to have made the scores arrive that morning. They were in the same room in Chauncey House where they'd gathered seven months before. Most of them, as well as spouses like Sylvia Mitchell of the Mass. General VD clinic, looked older, poorer, even less sure they'd done the right thing coming to Cambridge.

But not Artie. He was standing almost tall in his Brooks Brothers suit, and the only time he put his hand into one of its pockets was to give a satisfying tap to the slip of paper with his test results. He knew he was no longer some underdressed *arriviste* in this crowd. He stayed by the punch bowl, not fearing he might overturn it but hoping that someone would come up and congratulate him on acing the exams.

"Well, don't you look like the preppy who swallowed the goddamned canary," Elizabeth said, offering him a pig in a blanket. "Here. Take. But be warned: I think they're from the same batch they had in October."

"No, thanks," said Artie. "How was your nap?"

"Deep and fulfilling."

"Where's Richard?"

"You mean where's Downing. Now look, squirt, I ran into her outside. She was looking for a parking space for the Nazimobile. She's with a date. So why don't you forget about her and have a good time?"

"Sure," said Artie, looking down at his shined oxfords. "Really, where is Richard?"

"Give him another hour or two. Have you taken a look at Branded?"

"Yeah," said Artie. "He seems kind of lost."

"I think he blew one or two of the sections Canker didn't grade. Maybe he'll bail out and head for Yale. Then you and Downing'll have a clear field to be Richard Ellmann and Helen Gardner."

"Oh, c'mon," Artie said, just as he looked up and saw Angela come in with someone he recognized as the GQ cover she'd been with at Landon's Inn during the Saturday Night Massacre.

"Oh, Christ," he whispered.

"Relax," Elizabeth ordered. "Okay, he's good looking. Okay, let's be truthful. I'd sell my soul for a few seconds of heavy petting with him. But he's probably superficial. Couldn't score a six on the Renaissance."

Artie laughed. "Thanks. Oh, no, they're coming toward us."

"Well, hello," Angela said to him after she'd kissed Elizabeth. "I understand you did extremely well on the little tests. Congratulations. This is Henry Williams."

"Nice to meet you," Artie said before turning his attention back to Angela. "I understand you did extremely well too."

"Reasonably so," she replied. "I'd have done a bit better if the American literature summary from which I studied had been a bit more cogent."

Artie's mouth dropped. Was she kidding? "That summary," he said firmly, "was a perfect—"

He was interrupted by excited cooing. "Yes, *perfect*," said Little Nell, inserting herself into the circle. "That's what this is. A *perfect* occasion with *perfect* company. Please let me present my husband to you."

"It is a great pleasure and privilege to meet you," said Rodrigo, who had a heavy accent. He extended his hand to Angela. "I hope that the preceding year has not been excessively painful for you."

"Not at all," she said. "Only *stimulatingly* so. After all, when it comes to learning, as to anything else, one can't, as the saying goes, make an omelet without breaking a few eggs."

"Yes," Rodrigo said. "Beating them. Shattering them."

"Well," said Angela, "we'll see you all later." She propelled Henry away from the group, and Little Nell spirited Rodrigo toward further introductions.

"Elizabeth?" Artie said.

"Yeah?"

"I have two things to say. One is that Henry is a dorky name. Two is that I'm going to get drunk."

Elizabeth scowled. "Awright, if you gotta, you gotta. But not so drunk that you'll barf during the movie."

"What movie?"

"*Night of the Living Dead*, that's what movie. It's at the Orson Welles at midnight and we're going. Don't disappoint me. The prospect of this has kept me going for three weeks."

Night of the Living Dead depicts the implacable pursuit of human flesh by a group of recently resurrected ghouls in rural Pennsylvania. A Cambridge cult classic, it is especially popular around exam period, and Artie wasn't going to deny its pleasure to Elizabeth. But he hadn't counted on her sweeping up a whole theater party as twelve o'clock neared and they were leaving Chauncey House. When they got to the Orson Welles, their row of seats included Richard, Angela, Henry, Little Nell and Rodrigo, even Jeffrey Stanhope. Artie was sandwiched between Angela and Elizabeth. They talked over him.

"Watch close," Elizabeth said. "This little kid's gonna start gnawing on her father's arm."

Most of the audience was stoned. They greeted scenes like the intestinal barbecue with exaggerated terror or wondrous passivity, depending on what they'd taken. Artie took a few hits from a joint Richard produced.

"Oh, goodie!" exclaimed Angela when a particularly sweet-natured young woman was bitten by one of the fiends. "Can't imagine what took them so long to get to her."

Artie thought of going for broke, making a commando grope of her thigh, but there didn't seem much point to this since she wasn't even speaking to him. She'd pass the popcorn and the joint, but that was it. He was annoyed, woozy and bored. He'd already seen *Night of the Living Dead* at Brown, with Shane. The sight of the stiffs slurping hacked-off femurs like Popsicles just didn't do it for him anymore. He fell asleep and dreamt. Not of vampires and bones, but of moats and maidens, a medieval dream that probably resulted from thinking, on his way to the theater, about Angela's summary of that period, and whether or not his American one had really been deficient.

He knew the dream's landscape, could have drawn a map of it for any examiner who wanted one. He was looking for a rose, and there were three obstacles in his way: a river, a wall, a hedge. It was a crowded place, with people chatting in octosyllabic couplets and hopping allegorically about. Willard was chasing a jeweled fish with a golden net; Jeffrey Stanhope was in armor, on a white charger, ignoring the ladies offering him favors; Shane had a loaf of bread, a jug of wine and his hand in somebody's bodice. Rodrigo was spinning Little Nell on a catherine wheel outside a chapel in which Canker and Branded were illuminating manuscripts.

Elizabeth stood guard at the river through which Willard's shiny fish was swimming. She warned Artie not to pursue the rose any farther:

Forget her, hie back to your book;
She'll only treat you like a schnook.

But he went on to the next obstacle, the wall, startling Richard, who had been asleep at his post:

If you must, pursue this bubble;
But can love be worth the trouble?

He continued on to the hedge that was the final barrier between himself and the rose. Mrs. Crangel, in a pointed white and orange hat, sat upon a longhorn steer and said:

Lover, yours is an easy task:
If you want her back, just go ask.

He hopped the hedge and began calling, "Rose! Rose!" until he felt a poke in the ribs. "Show's over, squirt." The lights were up and everyone was leaving.

15

So you were the last person I saw in the dream."

"And I was speaking poetry?" Mrs. Crangel asked.

"Octosyllabics. They're easy."

"Let's go back to the unpoetic line we were talking about first. About how you never made 'some fucking effort to find out' about her. Do you think that's true?"

"Yes, I do. Sure she was mysterious. But how hard did I try to solve her? I'd ask her these questions, blanket open-sesame inquiries, and when she resisted, I'd just go back to nattering on about myself. Now I've got to leave town for the summer. I'll never find out. I don't even know where she is. Probably with her J.D. dreamboat. I'll bet she never comes back. Not if she's as bored as she said she was."

"But you know now that you want her. Isn't that important?"

"I suppose so. But I don't have her. And you think she's a bitch."

"That's beside the point," Mrs. Crangel said.

"What about this point, an old point: what if I just *think* I love her? What if I only need her?"

"No difference. Admit it, Arthur. Need and love are the same thing. Not in Plato's world, maybe, and maybe not in the *Romance of the Rose*, but here on the dirty earth, sure enough. Go home to Long Island and think about it."

"Can I call you if I go crazy again?"

"You never were crazy. Here's the number I'm at in the summer." She handed him a slip of paper, which he fiddled with as he started to make an embarrassed good-bye.

"Why," she suggested, "don't you put the number in one of your pants pockets? There's nothing else in them anymore."

"Hey," said Artie. "Thanks for everything."

Freddie was giving him a ride to Long Island. He had to have his stuff packed and out of Comus by noon. Tossing clothes and books into boxes from Star Market, Artie saw his Greek text flip open as it landed on top of a pile. "Cheer up, sweetie. See you at five-thirty," said the old note in the margin.

As soon as he and Freddie pulled out into Oxford Street, he asked, "So did you come up with anything on this Henry Williams?"

"Yeah," said Freddie, "but you're not going to like it, Dunnie. I talked to a three-L I know, a fellow Alabamian. He roomed with Henry Williams two years ago. When he met him, he said, 'Hey! I'm rooming with Hank Williams!' To which Henry Williams replied, 'Who's Hank Williams?' I tell you this so you'll remember when I tell you the rest that you're dealing with an asshole."

"Okay," said Artie, "what's the rest?"

"He just got a job with Exxon and they're sending him to Abu Dhabi, one of those pissant little Gulf states, at the end of June. His salary's going to have more digits than some folks have fingers. And he's going around telling people he's met a 'swell lady'—he talks like that. An asshole, I told you, remember that—"

"Yeah, yeah," said Artie, "get to the point. What's he telling them about this 'swell lady'?"

"That since upper-management A-rabs don't go for any fucking around or illicit cohabiting from the migrant workers, he's going to ask her to marry him."

On Long Island Artie regressed into the pampered postures of adolescence, its physical and psychic recumbency. He lay on the floor of his bedroom, watching television or listening to records. His mother came in with graham crackers and milk, pushing the reject button of the stereo if she found that he had fallen asleep.

He saw Angela receding like a dream into the blues and golds of a desert sunset.

Putnam Ave.
Cambridge
June 22, 1974

Dear Academic Star,

Thanks for your letter, which relieved my solitude. Absolutely nobody is around this place in summer.

I've got a job as a cab dispatcher until September. It's a good deal. I spend all day shouting into the short wave and telling these gorillas to keep their fucking shirts on or to cruise over to Central Square and pick up some old lady in front of Woolworth's. I'm saving money, enough so I may be able to move to better quarters when school starts. In the meantime, I'm able to afford the jumbo-size D-Con.

Sorry about her maybe going to Shoobie-Doobie, or whatever it's called. Don't make it overly shattering. If she goes, I want her to find me a sheik with plenty of petrodollars. If Omar Sharif can kiss Barbra Streisand, it could happen to me too.

Richard writes. Remember the very Protestant-looking old flame he ran into in the Copley Plaza the night before the M.A. tests? He's working for her father in New York this summer. He must roll into the office around three each day. Want to take bets? I say he won't be back in September. You, I know, will be. See you then.

Love,
Elizabeth

P.S. I haven't heard from her. Really.

A day after Elizabeth's letter arrived, on the evening of June 26, Freddie called up from the law office of Sullivan and Cromwell in lower Manhattan, where he was interning for the summer.

"Still interested in info on Henry never-known-as-Hank Williams?"

"Not really," said Artie. "Well, yeah."

"Well, he's in town. And she's with him. Me and O'Donnell and a couple of guys were having drinks at the Harvard Club. And Williams knows O'Donnell and says hello and soon everybody's sitting and talking. This is the story. They're both hanging out at the club until Sunday the thirtieth. After that they're off to Europe and on to Abu Dhabi. This information was stated twice, with clear emphasis: 'We're here until Sunday afternoon. No later.' "

"Why is he so damned emphatic? What does he think it is to you?"

"Moot question, Dunnie."

"Why?"

"Because he didn't tell me. *She* did. Very clearly. Twice."

"So?"

"So use your brains, doofus. I gotta go."

For most of the next day, Thursday, Artie pondered Freddie's implication—that since Angela knew Freddie would pass him the information, she must want him to know her whereabouts and get in touch with her.

For what? To say good-bye? Or to listen to her repent, so he could then rescue her from Henry Williams? This last prospect was a nice fantasy, but Artie wouldn't allow himself to entertain it seriously. First of all, she could have called him herself instead of leaving it to roundabout chance. And besides, why should she have changed her mind? Here was Henry Williams offering her the plunder of Abu Dhabi. He couldn't offer her Upper Derby. She was probably already married. If she wanted to see him at all it was to say good-bye. And why should he put himself through that?

Besides, tomorrow was the twenty-eighth, and even though

Shane hadn't been in touch for months, that was the day he'd long ago promised to meet in New York. Artie was going to keep the date. It was a 500-to-1 shot, but just maybe Shane would be there, offering a secure retreat into the raffish, presexual, preprofessional past.

So in the morning, with however little expectation, he set out for the Frick Collection via the Long Island Rail Road and a long hike from Penn Station up to Fifth Avenue and Seventieth Street.

Shane was not there. Artie arrived at El Greco's portrait of Saint Jerome at 11:02 and found, as he had expected, no sign of him. He decided to wander about the place anyway. It was his favorite museum; nothing in it ever changed, and it gave him a secure feeling. He could count on the little Paduan horse and Rembrandt's *Polish Rider* to be exactly where they had been when he first came here, on a field trip in the fifth grade; the same place where they'd been during the lunch hours he spent here at sixteen, when he had a summer job on East Sixty-third Street. He used to eat a hot dog on the street and then come in here to cool off, wandering past old man Frick's beautifully bound collections of sturdy writers like Bulwer-Lytton, listening to the baronial slurp of the indoor fountain.

He made a halfhearted circuit of the mansion now, too blue over Shane's absence, not to mention Angela's proximity, to give it much attention. But before he left, he did stick his head into what he always thought of as the living room (and what he suspected the Fricks called something else)—sort of to say goodbye to the picture of Sir Thomas More.

And then he noticed something he hadn't seen when he'd been in the room a half hour before: a small folded paper tucked into the bottom left-hand corner of the frame that contained the impossibly elongated Saint Jerome. Artie looked around and saw no guard. He plucked the paper from the painting.

Urn Man,

Get your ass on the 6:50 from Grand Central to Poughkeepsie and then hitch over to the Exhaust in Wappingers Falls. That's right. It's a club, and the Nocturnal Emissions have a gig there tonight. It's a long story, but I split from Mild Bill's back in March and rounded up the old N.E.'s, and we've been jerking off, so to speak, since May. We've had some great gigs so far, mostly in places like steel towns in Pa. where Bigfoot greasers shout terms of endearment like "Get fucked!" to us up on stage. Café society it ain't. But it's better than Mild Bill's microchip collective. (Fuck him and his wedding tomorrow. I'm not going—you come up and spend the weekend.) In this particular phase of superstardom we do everything from setting up the chairs to stamping hands at the door. You can help.

It's 10:05—this joint has just opened—& I don't have another sec. I've got to get up there and do the above-mentioned shit. I blew into town at 2 A.M. last night after two weeks in Bigfoot land. I'm staying with a chick I used to b*l* and am feloniously borrowing her car to get to W.F. and join the N.E.'s.

Get your butt up there.

Shane

Artie spent the next several hours walking around the upper East Side. He refused to go west of Fifth or south of Fifty-Seventh lest he get too close to the force field he imagined emanating from the Harvard Club. The 6:50 ran late, and by the time he arrived at the end of the line and secured a ride from a grandmother traveling between Poughkeepsie and Wappingers Falls, the Nocturnal Emissions were into their second set.

Shane was gyrating in a blue spotlight, playing lead guitar and singing his own lyrics, which it's true were not the sort likely to catch on fast in Clairton, Pennsylvania:

Baby leaves me frustrated when she puts up a fuss;
I go home all horny, just like old Priapus.

He had not exaggerated the trappings of his celebrity. The Exhaust was an atrocious dump whose patrons were mostly bristle-bellied truckers in their thirties escorting fallen nymphs of about seventeen, most of whom were screeching with knowledgeable lubricity over Shane's sweat-coated movements. Seating himself at a corner table and ordering a Bud, Artie waited for the band to take a break.

As soon as they did, Shane came over to his table and gave him a hug.

"Shane!"

He looked older.

"Urn Man."

Pause.

"Well, JK. Whatcha been doin'?"

"I'm out of school. I'm at my parents' house." Even though he knew the answer from his note, Artie could only think to repeat Shane's question. "What have *you* been doing?"

"Dope. And these gigs."

"Are you okay?" Artie asked.

"Yeah, Jack. I'm okay. Now that I'm out of the Sillycunt Valley."

"What are you going to do now?"

"Hey, man, do you have to ask? Just look around. Who wouldn't jump at perks like these? What a future!"

Artie noticed two things in Shane's face and voice—worry and bitterness—that he'd never noticed before. Were they temporary? "What about school?" he asked. "Are you going to go back to Brown?"

"Nah," said Shane. "No bucks, remember? You don't think Brother Bill is gonna give me a music scholarship, do you?"

"No," answered Artie, seeking refuge in the literal. "I guess not."

"How about you, Jack? What happened to Fanny?"

"You mean Angela?"

"Yeah, the Downing job."

"She's about to become the queen of the Arabian Peninsula."

"Since when the fuck have you been whimsical?" Shane asked. "Anyway, how's Hah-vad?"

"I did really well," Artie told him. "I actually cleaned up on the big tests."

"Gee, my goddamned heart may stop from the shock," Shane replied. "How about teaching the little pubies? Did you like it?"

"I really did," said Artie, about to launch into a high-speed monologue. "At first I didn't think I was going to be able to do it, but then, you know, I started my first class and—"

Shane put a hand over his mouth. "Later, Jack. After the show. Right now I just want the important bulletins. What about these demons you told me about? These little Kafka films running in your head."

Artie smiled. "They're gone." He realized his smile was a proud one, that he now believed their departure had been effected more by his own force of will than by any mysterious grace.

Shane hugged him hard. "I always told you you were a tough guy, Urn Man. Practically made of Pyrex."

The band's break ended when a member of the Exhaust's Friday-night clientele shouted, "Play some fuckin' songs!" In the next set some Chuck Berry numbers went over well with the truckers and their mini-molls, but Shane's own compositions continued to prove annoyingly cryptic. Fortunately, the crowd became increasingly drunk and doped, its good will increasing as its musical discrimination declined. The Nocturnal Emissions were called back for additional sets, and Artie ordered additional Buds.

They never made him drunk, though. It was almost as if they *were* being poured into Pyrex instead of susceptible flesh. Something new in him, something hard, wasn't letting him surrender to Shane's psychedelic lullaby. It was another siren song he was hearing, one coming up from the south, seventy-five miles away;

it was hers. If he was exchanging one dependence, one need—read "love"—for another, maybe so, but he could no longer feel dependent on Shane, who seemed suddenly so careworn, a drifter. Was he one of the tambourine men whose demise Angela had predicted months ago in Brooks Brothers? Was it possible that he, Artie, was in fact the one equipped to come through this new decade?

Artie realized that even without Angela he had, since the tests, become accustomed to feeling like a winner. Even more important, he knew that's what he wanted to be. He also knew that he wanted her, knew it for certain when he was out in the parking lot and starting to walk toward the bus station. Shane had always left him without warning, in response to the *Zeitgeist*'s latest induction notice. He couldn't feel guilty for doing the same. This decade's *Zeitgeist* might be less stormy than the last one's, a stale breeze by comparison, but Artie was going to catch it.

As he reached the end of the Exhaust's parking lot, the music of the Nocturnal Emissions was just a faint bass roar. It reminded him of something—the way the College Green at Brown had sounded from the storm shelter of B-level during the strike. When he'd been reading Keats and waiting for Shane.

But he kept walking toward the bus station.

"Sir," the clerk said, "it's after three in the morning. I'll repeat: if you wish to have me ring Mr. Williams's room, I'm willing to do so. But I cannot tell you whether he's with someone. No matter who you are and no matter who she may be."

So at 3:15 A.M. Artie found himself on West Forty-fourth Street, leaning against a railing a couple of buildings away from the Harvard Club and wondering what to do. He could go back home and return to the city tomorrow; after all, according to what Angela had told Freddie, she'd be there for another thirty-six hours. But if he went home he might lose his nerve, rethink the situation into emotional stasis. If he couldn't bring himself to ring Henry Williams's telephone at this hour, he'd never get back on the Long Island Rail Road tomorrow.

What would she think if he just rang the room? That he was at last a take-charge kind of guy, or just an absurd nuisance?

Ask her, he thought, realizing that it was she, right now, coming toward him. Or was it? It looked like Angela's silhouette walking west from Fifth Avenue, but some things were wrong. Her walk was too slow, humble somehow, and her hair, passing under the streetlamp, wasn't as blond as usual. But as she got closer, he knew for sure that it was she. Why had she lost her glow? Why could he tell, even in the dark, that she was somehow tarnished? Had everyone, not just Shane, lost power tonight?

She recognized him, walked up to him, stopped. Then he noticed that she hadn't just lost an aura. She was literally blackened. Her hair had streaks of soot in it, her face was smudged and puffy, her blouse was a mess.

She appeared defenseless in a way he'd never seen her, even at a loss for words, until she snuffled, "It blew up."

"Your relationship?" Artie guessed.

"No," she said, with no hint of a lilt. "The car. You were right. One gallon of gasoline equals fourteen sticks of dynamite."

"My God! Were you in it?" He took her by the arm.

"Don't be an idiot," she replied, recovering a bit of sting. "If I'd been in it, I'd be coming to you through a sieve. I'd just parked it and gone a few steps. I've been filling out forms in a police station for an hour. The officer was talking to me about loose wires and leaks and sparks, and I was giving him a theory about spontaneous combustion based on a reading of *Bleak House*. I'm sure he thought I was mad." She began to cry again, just a little. He put his arm around her and they walked silently for a couple of blocks, until he asked, "Why didn't you call him?"

"Call who?"

"Call Henry."

"Oh, Henry. We're fighting."

"You're fighting. Are you married?"

"No. I don't think purdah is good for rich white girls. He had some idea that I'd change my mind and do it en route, but I don't think so."

"Are you going at all?"

"No. I married an oil pump once. There doesn't seem any point in doing it twice. I don't know what about it began to bother me—the vulgarity, or possibly what your Mrs. Cringle would call a lack of 'growth.' "

"Kind of like going back under the wing of the freshman rock star who used to visit you in the library stacks."

"Darling," Angela said, "I'm sure what you said made perfect sense. That I don't comprehend a word of it now is just an indication that I'm a trifle disoriented. I'd like to sit down and eat something. And if you wouldn't mind, it'll be on you. My purse was in the front seat."

"Okay," said Artie, who noticed that they'd almost reached Ninth Avenue. "But I've only got nine bucks. And it's past three. It'll have to be a diner."

"I'm too tired to argue, darling."

But passing through the diner's door, Artie realized *he* was in the mood to argue. He took his arm away and said, sharply, "Why do you call me darling? You dumped me, remember?"

"So I did," she replied. "Just before those tests. Which you did spectacularly well on, you'll recall."

"What's the implication? That I did well because I was hurt?"

"Let's put it this way: being hurt didn't hurt."

"You dumped me for pedagogical reasons?"

"No," she said, very evenly, no lilt, no sting. "I dumped you because I was suddenly tired of you, because I was sick of your self-absorption, sick of everything being focused on your little woes, sick of your not seeing how I was in sadder shape than you. I kept waiting for the pot to see that the kettle was black. Don't you realize I spent the year every bit as screwed up as you?

Now there's a phrase to take the joy out of screwing," she said, losing herself in the laminated menu. They didn't say anything more to each other until the waitress had taken their orders.

"That's what you wanted?" Artie asked.

"The chicken pot pie? Under the circumstances—"

"No, I mean for me to realize that you were as screwed up as I was."

"Yes. For you to stop seeing me as a fantasy figure. But instead as someone who was in her own kind of trouble. Rich and bored and perfectly real, a stockbroker's daughter who made a smart—and stupid—marriage and a lot of other smart—and stupid—moves along the way. All right, a stockbroker's daughter who's exceptionally beautiful and frighteningly intelligent, but real nonetheless. I am not a figure of romance. I am not your fucking rose."

"How did you know about the rose?" Artie asked.

"Oh, you were murmuring through your dream in the theater. I heard you over the whimpers of the people having their flesh eaten."

"But why didn't you open up to me?"

"You mean when you asked your all-inclusive, computer-dating questions, the ones requiring perfectly unambiguous answers?"

"No, not then. Ever. Why did you *make* yourself a fantasy figure?"

"Because that's *my* problem. Just as you have all your little tics and fears. Which I tried to help you with as best I could."

Artie paused. "But why did you pick me? What was I to you? A science project? You once said you might have picked Richard. That he was 'perfectly presentable.' "

"I said 'might have screwed,' not 'might have picked.' There's a difference."

"But why pick me? I'm such a twit."

"Yes, but somewhat less so than before. Look at yourself." She pointed to the mirror against their booth. "You're different. Less foolish. More confident. You're not eating Jell-O. And you're eager, once we get our little troubles sorted out, to get back to Harvard and start being a success. Admit it."

"Yes. But I don't want all this Pygmalion business for the rest of my life. I don't want to be something you've constructed, like your medieval summary, which by the way was no better than my American summary."

"I haven't constructed anything. Speeded things up, perhaps. All I did was spot what was already there and coming. But last month I got tired of waiting to see you hatch. And what's all this 'rest of my life' nonsense?" She paused. "You know, if you were to speed up even a *little* more, get rid of the egg shell and goo and molt the feathers, I might be persuaded to love you, but as things stand— "

"I love *you*," he said, pushing aside her chicken pot pie and taking her hand.

"No, you don't," she said, taking it back. "All you do is worship me, and I'm sick of that. Life is *not* a romance. It's more like —if you bloody well must—a novel, a great big *realistic* three-decker, frantic with ambiguity and capable of turning out any number of ways."

"I want to be with you," he said.

"You want a guaranteed happy ending. And I'm not offering one."

"Are you offering anything?"

"A next installment. Perhaps. A chance to see how things come out. Lots of things. To see whether or not *you* get bored with *me*. To be together to see whether in a couple of years you still love your Keats more than you'll love success. And all that Irish professional-climbing you only think you're immune to—face it, darling, you've stepped up to their table and bought in. To see whether you'll still want me when I write better books than you, as I inevitably shall. To see whether you'll put up with all sorts of difficulties I'll continue to present, like being nasty to Mrs. Cringle in the street because I sometimes just can't help myself. That's what I'm offering you. The same thing I expect. A chance to keep reading. With the full realization that each of us may want to put the other's volume back on the shelf at some point."

"What is this? Membership in the Book-of-the-Month Club?" Artie asked.

"No, it's more like taking out a mortgage," she replied. "And seeing if one can keep up the payments."

Artie found the movement from literary to fiduciary metaphor arousing. "Can I repossess you?" he asked.

Angela was very tired. "Walk me back to the Harvard Club," she said. "I want to get my things."

He didn't go up to the room with her. He didn't want to witness a scene between her and Henry Williams, and even with all the new confidence she told him he possessed, he couldn't stand the thought of making a scene himself. So he just stood out on West Forty-fourth Street, his mind full of the risks and contingencies Angela had talked about. He didn't even know where they'd go. A hotel? For all her talk of mortgages, he still didn't own a credit card. It would be rough for however long it lasted, and his developing instincts made months seem more likely than years, but when he saw her again, coming out the door of the club and walking toward him in the lamplight, he knew what he had decided: to be, in love as in all else, an overachiever.